T0115153

OUT OF THE DARKNESS

INTO THE LIGHT

Mariann Fisette

iUniverse, Inc.
Bloomington

Out of the Darkness into the Light

iUniverse books may be ordered through booksellers or by contacting:

iUniverse
1663 Liberty Drive
Bloomington, IN 47403
www.iuniverse.com
1-800-Authors (1-800-288-4677)

ISBN: 978-1-4620-0183-5 (pbk)
ISBN: 978-1-4620-0184-2 (ebk)

Printed in the United States of America

iUniverse rev. date: 3/16/2011

CHAPTER 1

Neighbors and family tried to help the best they could but it was not enough, the up keep of the farmland and horses was to demanding with their busy lives. Betsey could not bear losing the farm that she and James had loved so much. A friend of Betsey knew of a farmhand named Joshua Tripp who might be able to help work the farm.

Sahara, Betsey's friend, would get in touch with him to call Betsey to set up a time to meet with her if she wanted. Betsey agreed to this and waited for his call. Several days had passed and no call so Betsey went to visit James at prison to break the bad news, as she may have to sell the farm. James was glad to see her, but knew something was very wrong! She tried to keep a smile sitting across from the man she thought would never leave her alone in this world. He knew she was very sad and asked her what was wrong.

Betsey began to cry, and told James about her problems; and how Sahara told her about the farmhand she had contacted but she had not heard from him. She still did not know how they could pay him anyway.

James took her hands in his and told her to wait a little longer before she put the farm up for sale. She agreed to hold off a little while longer and hugged her husband good-by again.

Chapter 2

Betsey left for her long drive home with deep sorrow in her heart. She arrived home 3 hours later to find a stranger on her front porch. She got out of her truck to a handsome man with coal black hair and eyes so green she got lost in them. He offered her his hand and introduced himself as Joshua. Betsey shook his hand and could not stop looking into those green eyes.

He proceeded to tell her he had been in the area and stopped to look at the farm. She explained that she could not pay him much, but could give him room and board with meals if that was suitable for him. He could not keep his eyes off her as well.

Betsey was a beautiful young red head with an hourglass figure. He wanted to run his hands through her long curls and kiss those plump ruby lips. Joshua told her he had a job to finish first but could start next week, if that was fine with her. Betsey could not contain her excitement and told him that would be fine.

She could not wait to let Sahara know he was hired. She quickly went into the house to call her. Sahara was thrilled for her and said she would stop by tomorrow to see her. Betsy hung up with her and headed to the barn to feed the horses. She was flying on a cloud as she fed the horses knowing they could keep the farm for now.

What she did not know is the horrid events coming to their farm!

Chapter 3

It was next week, Joshua was arriving today, and it was a cold February day. Betsey was busy early that morning baking fresh bread and donuts with a skip in her step, which had been gone for some time now. She was so happy they could keep the farm for now.

She could not wait for her next visit with James to give him the good news. Betsey missed him more and more as the days had gone by. It had been 1 month since he had gone to prison now. She had managed to run the farm, but could not on her own any longer.

Betsey, whom was left the farm by her parents along with an inheritance to help keep the farm running which was almost gone now due to lawyer fees for her husband's trial, there was a knock at the front door. She opened the door and there stood Joshua. He remarked about the unbelievable smells coming from inside.

Betsey blushed and invited him in. She brought him into the kitchen, as she was ready to take the bread out of the oven. He gasped at the smell of the kitchen as he sat at the kitchen table with the bread and donuts cooling on racks in front of him. Betsey asked if he was hungry. He said he had not been, but sure was now. She offered to cook him some eggs to go with the bread and donuts. He was thrilled and accepted.

Betsey sat and ate with him and talked about the farm over coffee. Breakfast was done; time to show him the barn. They walked down to the barn and he took in the estate he would be living on. Joshua's head was wheeling on how he would run this farm as his own he thought. Betsey was very impressed with the ideas he had on running the farm and how to turn it around to profit from it. She trusted him and enjoyed the company.

Chapter 4

Things took off well between the two of them. He worked the farm and Betsey was able to get back to teaching at the middle school, as she had in the past. Things were going well, she was teaching again and he was running the farm like her dad had.

One day she came home from work to find a sign at the end of their estate stating hayrides and horse training at the Salem's Trail Farm. Betsey asked Joshua about the Salem's Trail Farm sign and he told her he is trying to upgrade the farm to make some money.

She went inside to prepare dinner that night. Her head was wheeling with the thought of strangers being on their farm. She prepared a gourmet dinner with beef and fresh veggies stir-fry style. They totally enjoyed their meal and enjoyed wine hours after with dessert. It had been the best night for her and him in a long time. It was getting late so he went to the barn were he slept in a small room in the back of the barn. Betsey headed upstairs to her and her husband's room, which looked out over the estate. He settled in quickly and felt at home. She tossed and turned all night not knowing if she had made the right choice, regarding the farm. She had a real draw toward him.

Morning came quick and Betsey was in the kitchen getting breakfast ready for her and him. Joshua appeared looking so bold in his tight fitting jeans and short sleeve white shirt. He was wearing a cowboy hat designed for royalty and boots men around here would die to have.

They finished breakfast and she headed for school, he for the barn and horses. His day had been great; he had his own horses and miles of fields, he thought. She enjoyed being back at school with her kids. Betsey's day was great, her class was getting ready for spring; it had been a long hard winter.

She was having her class make flowers and leaves to decorate the hallways and classrooms. Her life could not be better at this time. Betsey was planning to visit James this weekend. She was so excited to tell him they could save the farm, with her going back to work and Joshua running the farm.

The weekend came and Betsey headed off for her 3-hour trip to see James. Joshua sent her off with his breakfast of bacon, pancakes and eggs. She enjoyed someone else cooking for her. She headed out at 8am that morning. She arrived at the prison at 11am. James was anxiously waiting for her arrival.

Betsey greeted her husband and was so full of excitement. She told him about Joshua's ideas on running the farm. James was ok with Joshua running the farm. James thought this would bring in money, which they needed. They hugged and she left again for her 3-hour ride home.

When she arrived home, he had a great dinner ready for her. Joshua had cooked Jambalaya and had wine chilling. She was so glad she did not have to cook. They sat down to a great meal and conversation. They both said their goodnights and went to bed. The morning came quick for both of them.

CHAPTER 5

Betsey rose earlier to prepare breakfast. It was full of biscuits, eggs, and homemade honey. Betsy left again for work. As the day was fading, Joshua noticed a girl watching the farm. It was Sahara's daughter Alexis. Joshua approached the girl with a hello and extended his hand to her. She took his hand and shook as introducing herself to him.

He smiled and said; boy, this part of the country sure has pretty girls. Alexis blushed and thought he was so handsome.

He asked her what brought her out this way. She replied she had to give a book to Betsey from her mother. He told her Betsey was not home from work yet but he would give it to her. Alexis gave him the book and headed for home giggling on how cute he was. Joshua headed into the house with book in hand. He was done with work on the farm for today.

Joshua had a great dinner in mind to prepare for him and Betsey. As soon as he entered the kitchen, he began preparing the veal he had marinating in the refrigerator. Joshua put olive oil in a cast iron pan and heated it up then added veal with spices to sear it. He had a pot boiling for pasta. After turning the veal, he added crushed black pepper, sea salt, and rosemary to the water. As his meal was cooking, he set the table for supper. He brought out the good china and lit the candles. Everything was going well with dinner; the aroma was wonderful.

It was 6 o'clock; Betsey should be home soon now. Joshua had gotten all cleaned up and smelling good. As he added the last touches to dinner, Betsey came thru the door. Betsy was stunned by the beautiful smells coming from her kitchen. Joshua greeted her with a glass of wine and a smile. She took the glass of wine and entered the kitchen telling him she could really get used to this. He laughed and told her he enjoyed cooking. It was his passion.

They sat for hours after eating, enjoying a bottle of wine and great conversation. As he got up to clear the table, she told him no she would do it. He made a beautiful meal; she would at least do the dishes. He followed her into the kitchen; he would dry the dishes at least. They laughed and really enjoyed each other's company.

It was late; time for bed, morning would come fast. As Betsey headed up to bed, she thought how great the last two days had been. She not only had help with the farm but great company as well. It put a smile on her face, which she missed. Joshua headed for his room in the barn smiling all the way. He too had enjoyed his past two days at the farm. However, what Betsey was unaware of was he never planned on leaving!

CHAPTER 6

The morning brought snow so Betsy would be home today. School would be closed due to the storm. Betsey was in the kitchen preparing a soufflé for breakfast with homemade biscuits with honey. Coffee was brewing as Joshua came thru the kitchen door. He was raving about the smell in the kitchen. Betsey told him it is the least she could do after his two great dinners and laughed.

She told him to sit down at the table and brought him a cup of cinnamon coffee freshly brewed. He took a sip and smiled, the best cup of coffee he ever had. She was pleased. Breakfast was ready. They sat and ate over conversation on what to do on the farm, as Betsey could help while being home from work. Joshua had started running new fencing along the back quarter of the farm to extend room for the horses to run. She would help him finish the fencing then. He remembered Alexis's visit, went, and gave the book to her. She took the book and laughed.

She had lent it to Sahara one year ago on cooking for dummies. She guessed it helped as the last meal she had there was edible. She headed up stairs to take a shower and get dressed for outside work. He cleaned up the kitchen and dreamed how beautiful she must look in the shower. They headed for the back quarter of land with snow falling. He was glad to be able to spend the day with her. She aroused him as no other woman had!

She looked hot in her overhauls fitting every curve of that beautiful body. Skin the color of milk. Her blue eyes sparkled and danced in the snowflakes, like sapphires. He was unable to take his eyes off her as they worked. They finished up just before lunchtime.

They worked up an appetite and were wet and cold. They started heading for the house when they saw a car approaching the farm. It was Sahara's car. They reached the house laughing as they threw snowballs at each other the whole way. When they reached the driveway, they were soaked in snow. Sahara got out of her car in disbelief on how her friend was so happy, laughing and full of snow. Betsey greeted her with a big hug.

She introduced her to Joshua. They all went inside to get out of the cold. Betsey headed for the kitchen and put on a pot of water for tea. She told them to have a seat in the living room. They all sat and Sahara began on how great Betsey looked. Talk went to the ideas Joshua had for turning the farm into a moneymaker.

He planned on opening it up to sleigh rides and horseback riding. In addition, in the spring cook outs and events of fishing derbies at the back pond along with barrel ridding for the locals. Betsey loved the ideas as well as Sahara. The future of the farm was looking up.

Then in the fall, there will be spooky hayrides and pumpkin carving contests. Sahara had to leave to pick up Alexis at a friend's house. They all said goodbyes and Betsey walked her to her car. She hugged Betsey and told her how glad she was for Joshua coming into her best friends' life. Betsey went back into the house to find him washing up cups and plates and smiled. I do not know if I can get use to the unbelievable fortune that has come to me!

He reached for her hand and asked her to go for a night out? She asked where; he replied just trust me! You will not be sorry you did. Betsey agreed and went to change clothes. As she went upstairs, she thought where we are going. She did not know what to wear. She came back down the stairs to find him at the bottom of the stairs. A little shocked to see him there, she asked where we are going.

He smiled and told her to dress casual. She smiled and headed back up stairs.

CHAPTER 7

He knew of a great place in downtown Salem to eat. It was an Indian restaurant well known by many. It was close to the waterfront and would be great for an after dinner walk or carriage ride.

He went to the barn to change his clothes as well. When he returned to the house, she was dressed in tight blue jeans and a hot black velvet top. Her long curly red hair draped down her back! He stopped in his tracks seeing her. She was amazed at how good he cleaned up. He was handsome in black jeans and a vest. She did not know how long his hair had been until now. She liked it!

He asked if she was ready to leave. She said yes and they headed for his truck. She asked him where they were going. He told her and she was thrilled. She told him that she always wanted to try India West restaurant. He was glad!

They arrived at the restaurant; he parked, and got out to open her door for her. She got out as he grabbed her hand to escort her to the door. Joshua and Betsey were seated at a table near the window. It was perfect. They ordered and enjoyed the food and great conversation again. They left the restaurant and walked along the waterfront filled with lights and laughter of other couples. It was a wonderful night.

They came across a horse carriage and took a ride thru the streets of Salem. It was the best night Betsey had in many years. Joshua could not remember having a better time. He still could not take his eyes off her. They headed for the truck; it was after ten o'clock and cold. The hour ride home was fun, they sang with the radio all the way home.

It was 11:30 when they reached the farm. They entered the house and could not believe the temperatures outside. The snow had stopped but the wind had picked up. It was 10 below zero. She was worried about him sleeping in the barn tonight. Betsey offered for Joshua to sleep on the couch in the house. He took her up on that offer. She was relieved he agreed to sleep in the house. She told him to make himself comfortable and went upstairs to change.

Joshua went into the kitchen to prepare a nightcap. He found some left over biscuits and added hot caramel over them, grabbed two glasses and a bottle of brandy. He returned to the living room to find her sitting on the couch with a great purple velvet jumpsuit on. She was glowing! She thought what he had brought was a lovely ending to a perfect night.

They sat and talked, laughed and went over the plans for the farm. They both could not keep their eyes off each other, sparks! It was 2 am already and time to go to sleep. They were not tired at all. However, they knew morning would be upon them soon enough. They did not want the night to end! Betsey started to head up stairs, when he stopped her and kissed her. She was like putty in his hands. It escalated to the bedroom where they made love for hours. They both feel asleep and slept until late morning.

Joshua woke up first and headed for the kitchen. He began to prepare breakfast; fried goat cheese on spinach leaves with tomatoes and a light olive oil dressing. He was just getting a bottle of champagne to open when Betsey came into the kitchen.

She gave him a hug and kiss; he grabbed her and kissed her long and hard. She loved the feeling, but was still feeling guilty about James. She was amazed with his breakfast! They sat close, ate, and drank for hours.

It was a Saturday so Betsey did not have to go to school. They returned to the bedroom for round two of lovemaking. When they could not move anymore, they went to the shower, which ended up with more lovemaking. Finally, they got dressed and planned their day of getting the farm ready for the public events planned. The opening date was only three weeks away. Betsey also was renaming the farm. Its' new name was going to be Mainstay Bed and Breakfast Inn.

She planned to quit her teaching job to run the Inn. Joshua would run the horse rides and rodeo events on the farm.

CHAPTER 8

It was the end of February, lots to do. Betsey called Sahara as she worked for the newspaper in town. She wanted new Mainstay Bed and Breakfast adds in the paper. Sahara would get it into next print.

She invited Sahara and Alexis to dinner that night. Betsey and Joshua worked together to cook a great meal for them. The meal was great and they all enjoyed the company. Much conversation was on the new opening of Mainstay Bed and Breakfast. Sahara and Alexis could not wait for the opening. They were helping with the advertising of the opening day.

As they were leaving, Sahara pulled Betsey aside and told her she never looked better! They both winked at each other and laughed and they left. Joshua and Betsey cleaned up the kitchen and headed up to bed together. It was only sleep tonight for them both.

Betsey awoke early and was feeling bad about sleeping with a man she hardly knew! Then there was her husband. She had been unfaithful so this was confusing for her. She got up at five o'clock, took a shower and headed downstairs to try to clear her head. The best way to do this was cooking in her kitchen.

She was making home fries, bacon, Cheddar cheese omelets and homemade bread in the oven. Coffee brewed and smelled good. Joshua was awoken by the smells coming from the kitchen. He went into the shower and then headed downstairs to the great smell of food. He noticed she was crying. He went to her, hugged her, and asked what was wrong.

She told him nothing, just sit and have some breakfast. He knew something was definitely wrong! He took her hand and she pulled away and started to cry. He got up and held her as she wept.

He kissed her and told her everything would be fine. Betsey felt better in his arms. They finished breakfast and headed out to feed the horses and get to work on finishing the work for opening day.

They fed the horse's new hay and headed out to finish the fencing for the trail rides. It was almost noontime and they had finished with the fence. Betsey was going to head up to the house to start lunch; Joshua would start running lights on the trees near the barn. Betsey was preparing potato soup with leeks and bacon along with a BLT wrap for lunch. Lunch was ready so she rang a bell for Joshua to come up to the house.

It was now 1: 30 and both were very hungry after their morning work. Joshua cleaned up and sat at the kitchen table to a most delicious lunch! He raved how good it was. He said their guests would not want to leave after tasting her cooking. They both laughed. They both cleaned up after lunch and headed back out to work.

Joshua had almost finished the lighting, only one tree left. They both finished the last tree and were delighted with the results. It was time to bring the horses in to the barn for nighttime. They called the last horse in and began night feeding of fresh hay and water. As Betsey was tossing the last bale of hay in the stall, he grabbed her from behind and tossed her in to the leftover hay in the next stall. They were rolling around laughing, when they heard a voice-calling hello.

It was Sahara and Alexis bringing the new signs for the farm for their new venture. One sign read Mainstay Bed and Breakfast and the other Hay Rides and Horseback Riding. Betsey was pleased with the signs. Joshua had already installed the black wrought iron poles for the new signs. They all went to the road to hang the new signs at the entrance to Main Stay Inn.

It was approaching dinnertime now and Betsey had venison marinating in the icebox, along with fresh cucumbers in oil, sugar and parsley. They invited them to stay for dinner and Sahara and Alexis agreed to stay. Joshua got the grill going for the meat. Betsey and the girls set the table for dinner and opened a bottle of wine to breath. The venison steaks were ready and they all sat down to eat. The meal was a success and was encouraged to be included on the bed and breakfast menu. This was not, or been considered yet for the guests staying at the Inn.

Betsey and Sahara made plans to start the menu tomorrow. It would take a couple of days to be printed. Betsey was so overwhelmed with what yet had to be finished, with time running out. They all advised her everything would go well. It was late so Sahara and her daughter headed home.

Betsey and Joshua cleaned up after supper and retired to the living room for another glass of wine before heading to bed. It had been a great day! Tomorrow would be for planning menus for the guests staying at Mainstay Inn.

Three courses had to be thought out carefully per day, per week to people's preferences. They headed up to bed knowing with all left to do, not much sleep was in hand for the two!

Sleep was hard but achieved that night. Morning came quick and opening day would be coming soon. It was a beautiful morning, chilly but the sun was out warming things up nicely. Betsey was up first, showered, and dressed. She headed downstairs to start breakfast as Joshua took his shower.

She prepared cheese, asparagus, and tomato omelets. Joshua came downstairs and asked what smelt so good. Betsey laughed and told him what was for breakfast. They ate and talked over the first week's menu for the inn. They mulled over many combinations of meals to serve. As they narrowed down to three meals a day, Betsey entered them into her laptop.

CHAPTER 9

They were off to town to shop for food needed for the menus. Their first stop was Birmingham Family Market in down town Salem. Betsey had known the family as a child. Carl Birmingham's son Todd and his wife Samantha ran the store, as Carl passed away 2 years prior.

Betsey introduced Joshua and handed Todd the list of meats she would need wrapped up for her first week's meals planned. As Todd was getting her order ready, they collected all the fruit and produce needed as well. Birmingham Market had the freshest meats and produce on the island.

As they were waiting for their meats, they talked with Samantha about the changes to the farm. She was so excited for Betsey and her new business adventure and wished her well. Betsey asked if she could post a flyer in their storefront window for Mainstay Inn. They would be pleased to do so! Joshua went out to the truck to get one of their posters for Mainstay Inn. When he returned, Samantha took it and put it in their front window.

Betsey paid for their supplies and thanked them for their help. They left Birmingham's and headed across town to Wendy's gourmet shop for imported olive oils and many different wines to cook with and serve with lunch and dinners. They entered Wendy's and Joshua was amazed at how beautiful the store was. Wendy greeted Betsey congratulating her on the new Inn.

It did not take long at all for news to travel in Salem! Betsey again introduced Joshua and handed her a list of oils and wines she needed. Wendy viewed the list and thought they were wonderful choices. She called her helper and gave the list to Tammy to gather everything for Betsey. As Tammy was filling her order, Wendy winked at Betsey and said way to go girl. Betsey blushed and laughed. Betsey asked Wendy about putting her poster in her front window for Mainstay Inn. She as well agreed to advertise for Betsey.

So again, Joshua went to get a poster for Wendy's store. Next stop was Bill's General Paper Goods. They bought large quantities of napkins, paper towels and toilet paper. Bill was pleased with her order and wished her well as they left the store. Last stop was Helen's Emporia Bath Shop at the waterfront shops. Helen greeted them at the door and could not contain her excitement on Betsey's new business adventure with Mainstay Inn. Joshua took Helen's breath away on how handsome he was. She gave Betsey thumbs up.

Without Betsey asking, Helen asked for her poster advertising her Inn to put in her front window. As Joshua went to get one Betsey could not control her feelings as to how kind the merchants had been in Salem to them today. Helen hugged her and told her they all wished her well with Mainstay Inn. As Betsey finished her order of soaps and shampoos for the Inn, she thanked Helen again for all her support. As they headed back home with all their goods, Joshua remarked on how nice the merchants were in town. She smiled and felt blessed on how the people of

Salem supported her in her time of need. She could not ask for a better place to live.

They arrived home and unpacked all the supplies from their shopping trip. After they put everything away, they were exhausted. Joshua offered to take Betsey back into town for a relaxing lunch. She accepted his offer. He asked her where she would like to have lunch. She said she would like to go to Nell's eatery and candy store on the waterfront. Betsey told him she had the best lunch spot in Salem.

Nell had a great catering business as well. They arrived at Nell's at 12: 00 it was busy with locals having lunch. They waited a ½ hour for a table, but it was worth the wait. As they waited, some of the locals stopped to congratulate Betsey on the Mainstay Inn and to meet Joshua her new farmhand. They finally were seated and placed their order, Nell's special of the day. It was a buffalo chicken and cucumber wrap with parsley and cucumber soup. Nell herself brought them their food. Betsey introduced Joshua to Nell and Nell started to tell him how Betsey and she were friends in school.

Betsey stopped her before she could embarrass her and filled her in on the new Mainstay Inn. Nell wished her well and said she would help in any way Betsey needed. Betsey then asked her if she would put her poster in the front window. Nell said of course, as Betsey asked for help preparing menus for her Inn as well. Nell was thrilled she wanted her help; Nell was so modest on how great she was with food.

They finished lunch, Betsey and Nell arranged to meet tomorrow at the farm to go over menus. Betsey was feeling more confident about cooking for the Inn with

Nell's help. Joshua had to laugh on how smart Betsey was. "You really are a good business women already" he laughed. She just smiled and said stick with me and we will go far as a team. You can definitely bring the outdoor activities with no problem, and me with the Inn it will be a success.

As they approached the driveway to Mainstay, they noticed several cars up near the barn. As they approached the people standing outside their cars, Joshua asked Betsey if she knew them. Betsey replied no, not at all. They approached the couples standing at the barn and introduced themselves to them. It was people on vacation from NY City who saw her posters in town and wanted to make a reservation for a summer stay at Mainstay Inn.

Betsey and Joshua were stunned at the prompt response to the posters. They proceeded to show them around the farm and then invited them into the house. The couples were very impressed with Mainstay. They confirmed a 2-week stay in July at Mainstay.

As the couples drove off Betsey and Joshua were in shock, all ready had four visitors for months in advance. This was going to be a great business deal for them both. They opened a bottle of wine to celebrate. As they sat down on the couch, a knock at the door. Betsey went to the door to see many friends from town on her doorstep.

As she went to the front door, Joshua was starting a fire in the large fireplace, as the sun was setting and it was getting cold out. Betsey was stunned at the many local friends stopping by to wish her well.

She hurriedly invited them in as temperatures were dropping fast outside. As they all entered the living room, they were stunned themselves as to how handsome Joshua was while tending to the fire with logs. Betsey stopped him from tending to the fire and introduced their company to him.

Joshua was a bit put out at the visitors, as he wanted Betsey to himself. She asked Joshua to open some more wine for their company as she instructed them to have a seat in the living room. She followed Joshua into the kitchen to prepare a platter of cheese, crackers, and grapes for their unexpected company.

As she reentered the living room, they all became silent with the gossip that had been going around the room. Betsey set the platter down on the coffee table and laughed is there anything on your minds! They all looked at each other, but no one spoke. Then Ethel started on how shocked they were that she had a strange man living with her as she was still married to James. All the others charmed in with Ethel's remarks.

Betsey laughed and tried to silence her company before Joshua returned with the wine. She explained her situation with the up keep of the farm while James was in prison and she almost had to sell if it had not been for Joshua's help. They all felt bad on how they had approached Betsey regarding her situation. She made them feel welcome and appreciated and all left loving the idea of Mainstay Inn. They all wished them well with opening day and said they would help if they were needed, just give a shout. Betsey said she would and said good-bye as they left the farm.

Joshua was brooding in the kitchen, as he never had her to himself as planned earlier. As she entered the kitchen, she heard him mumbling and asked what was on his mind. She surprised him as he was washing glasses from their guests. He broke a glass and cut his hand.

Betsey ran to help him and he pushed her away. She was shocked at his response to her.

His old habits regarding his real personality were showing and this was not good as for he would have to leave Betsey and Mainstay, as this had been the first place he had felt at home in many years.

She went to approach him again, to tend to his cut hand. He tried to compose his rage and let her help him. Joshua was feeling a delight with the sight of blood and its warm feeling in his hands. He put those thoughts away for now and let her bandage his hand. He composed himself and gave her a hug and kiss for taking care of him so lovingly.

They returned to the living room and fire that had been dwindling away without care. He added more wood and arranged the logs and soon the flames were going. They sat on the couch together and she asked him what had happened in the kitchen prior. He was embarrassed on how he had lost control. In addition, he apologized about his bad temper by telling her she was the most important person in his life and he would never hurt her. She told him she felt the same way.

They sat and watched the fire and drank wine as they went over what was yet to be finished for opening day. They still had to get the wagons ready for hayrides, polish the saddles for horseback riding and groom the horses. They would be able to finish this task tomorrow. Opening day would be soon.

Betsey was tired and said was heading up to bed. He agreed and followed her upstairs. They both undressed and got into bed. He was excited from earlier, when he saw and felt the blood from his cut. He wrapped himself around her, kissed her neck, and then moved down to her breasts. Betsey whimpered with pleasure and begged for more!

Joshua was so excited he indulged himself with her beautiful breasts and lost himself in her ruby red lips. They both were escalating into pleasures they never experienced before with another partner. They went through many stages and finished with full erotic pleasure. Sleep came soon for both.

CHAPTER 10

They awoke to sun streaming in through the windows at 6: o'clock am. Joshua reached and kissed her neck and said time to get up my princess. Betsey rolled over and kissed him gently on the lips. They should be getting up and going to feed the horses now, but other things were defiantly on their minds. They both indulged themselves in pleasures of the heart.

Then Betsey heard the whimpering of the horses. They needed to feed and let them out to pasture. She gently pulled herself from Joshua to shower and go tend to the horses.

This morning Betsey did not want to wake him after his bad hand cut last night and remembered his personality change. She left him sleeping and headed to the barn feeling confused on her part last night in bed. She almost felt drugged after last night's experience, amazing as it was!

She fed grain to the horses and was ready to get fresh water and hay when Joshua appeared. He startled her! Joshua approached her, kissed her, and asked, was last night as good for you as it was for me? She blushed and said yes, very much so.

They finished with the horses and headed for the house for breakfast. They were both famished after their love making the night before. They both got breakfast ready together. Pancakes, bacon, eggs, biscuits with honey, and fresh ground coffee cinnamon. They inhaled their breakfast to refuel their bodies for the day's work to come.

Breakfast was done and time to get things done for opening day. They headed for the pastures to check fencing. It all looked good, no problems there. Next was the building for guests and non-guests to sign up for hayrides and horseback riding lessons. It was repainted a week ago and now needed a touch of design. They had grape vines and mini lights to decorate the building as well. They also had to add shutters to the front windows of the check-in building for horse riding and hay rides.

Betsey had custom painted them in lavender to match the dark grey building. She also included black and cranberry sunflowers to the shutters. After they were in place, they strung lights around the roof and porch of the front of the building. Everything was almost ready for opening day.

It was heading towards noontime now. Betsey remembered she was due for a visit with James in prison today. It had almost slipped her mind. She told Joshua she had to leave for a visit with James. He was very upset that she was going to see her husband! After they have shared a bed and made love many times. He thought she was his and his only! He felt her response to him strongly and willingly. Why was she leaving him for a man that could give her nothing but pain?

Betsey said goodbye, see you later to night, and walked to her car. Betsey started her car, nothing happened, it did not start. She tried again, engine just growled, no spark. She got out and opened the hood of the car. James had taught her some things about cars and trucks {mechanically that is}. She could not find the problem at first sight.

It was cold and the wind was fierce biting at her hands, so she headed for the house to call the prison to let James know she would not be there due to car problems. Betsey was devastated she would not be able to see James for another month now. It was only monthly visits allowed for the prisoners at the prison.

Betsey came into the house to find Joshua planning a dinner party at the farm that night. He acted shocked to see her! She told him her car would not start. He said he would go out and check it out. He knew what the problem was regarding it not starting. Joshua had removed one spark plug it would take to start the car and replaced it with a bad spark plug. The car would not start with this bad spark plug. He was counting on Betsey not knowing this, it worked.

Betsey was on the phone with the prison warden to get the message to James when Joshua came back in the house. He gave her a look like he did not know why it would not start. She gave the warden the bad news and hung up the phone. Joshua tried to comfort her as she was crying as not to be able to see James for another month.

Joshua let her know about the surprise party he planned for this evening. She confessed she overheard him on the phone when she had entered the house. He continued to tell her who was coming and they needed to get ready for company. He thought it would bring her spirits up after not being able to visit with James. He so deceived her that day.

Joshua was controlling her life now and she had no clue. Joshua told her to go and change for their party. She was hesitant but complied. Everything was ready now for the party. He had finger food coming with Nell, wine coming with Wendy and her mate Jeff. The lights were all on surrounding the farm and it looked beautiful and inviting. Joshua had a fire roaring in the fireplace and many candles to give the living room a beautiful glow. He had included Todd and Samantha but they had a previous invite to attend to, but were sorry not to attend theirs. They asked for a rain check.

Betsey came downstairs looking more amazing than ever to him. She wore a blue velvet corset top with bleached tight jeans. She had knee high black suede boots on as well. Joshua was taken with her beauty. The doorbell rang and he told her to relax he would answer the door. She entered the living room and stopped, it was the most beautiful thing she had ever seen in her house. The fireplace mantel covered with fresh lavender and baby's breath, the whole room aglow with lavender candles, at least fifty of them. It smelled and looked right out of a fairytale book.

As she was looking in amazement, Wendy grabbed her and startled her. She turned around to see her long time friend hugging her. Surprise Betsey! They all were there now and enjoying the company, drink and food. All the gossip was about Betsey and Joshua. After the talk was finished with Betsey's new man, they ate, drank, and enjoyed the evening.

The last person to leave was Wendy, her school friend. She could not believe the change in her old friend {Betsey} and could not wait to see what would come next in her life. After Wendy left, Joshua took Betsey by the hand up stairs to bed. They could clean up in the morning. As they entered, the bedroom he grabbed her from behind, it startled her and she lost her balance. He caught her and laid her on the bed. They began kissing each other's bodies until it became full contact between the two. They made love again for hours before falling asleep.

CHAPTER 11

Morning had arrived earlier then Betsey wanted. She went to grab Joshua. He was already gone. She was up, so headed to the shower and there he was in the shower. She took off all her nightclothes and entered the shower with him. He was glad and welcomed her warmly!

They were in the shower for at least an hour, finally they decided to get out and dry off. Who was going to make Breakfast? One had to go feed and let the horses out yet. Joshua was already planning to take her to Nell's place for breakfast. He offered to go take care of the horses {as this was his job anyway}. She agreed and headed to get dressed, singing as she went. He loved the sound of that.

Joshua went to the barn and gave the horses new bedding and grain, as well as new water. It took him at least one hour before he came in the house. Betsey was mixing up batter for biscuits when Joshua entered the kitchen. He took her hand and told her to put the dough in the refrigerator as he was taking her out for breakfast. She would be ready to leave in five minutes.

As they drove into town, conversation was about things left for tomorrow's opening day. As they were running a checklist, sleigh was ready, barrels were ready around the pond for fires to warm the skaters, and lights hung around the barn, trees, and buildings. They had all the food needed for the cookout planned as well.

Betsey would have to stop at Brigham's to pick up apples to make candy apples that she forgot to get. They arrived at Nell's and went in for breakfast, busy as usual but were able to find a seat. Nell spotted them and came to their table. Hi, did not get enough of me yesterday! They all laughed as Betsey told her that her food must have made a big impression on Joshua, as he was here again. He laughed, said almost as well as Betsey's. They all laughed and ordered their breakfast with Nell.

Nell brought them goat cheese, mushroom, tomatoes, and basil omelets with honey biscuits and coffee. Nell asked what she could bring for opening day. Betsey told her just yourself. They left Nell's and headed across town to pick up apples. After getting the apples, Joshua said he would like to take a walk down to the waterfront. Betsey was thinking of everything to be done, and was hesitant to the walk. He told her they would have plenty of time to finish up things later and she agreed to some fun downtown.

They passed a store with jewelry of natural stones in the front window. Betsey stopped and was in love with a pink quartz ring, he noticed her eyes light up and the smile on her face looking at it. He asked her if she wanted it. She shrugged, told him she could not afford it with the Mainstay's opening. As they walked past a candy store, she said she needed to go in and get candy coating for the apples. Joshua said he would wait outside on the bench.

Betsey went into the store, he went back to the jewelry store and purchased the ring and hid it in his jacket pocket. When Betsey came out of the store, he was sitting on the bench with a smile on his face. She asked him what was next. He wanted to walk out to the lighthouse. They headed out to the lighthouse where the view was breathtaking. You could see all the way out to the breakers and all the sailboats in the cove. He gave her a big hug and told her how many feelings he was starting to have for her and kissed her cheek. Betsey blushed and kissed him back.

They decided they had everything needed for opening day and walked back to the truck to head home. As they arrived home, Sahara's car was in the driveway. They got out of the truck, Sahara and Alexis were sitting on the front porch. Betsey was glad to see them. They thought she could use some help for opening day. Betsey thanked them and said she sure could use the help. They all went into the house after putting stuff they had bought in town in the kitchen.

Joshua went out to get wood for the fireplace to take off the chill in the house. Sahara and Alexis sat in the kitchen with Betsey going over the menu for opening day. They were having venison burgers stuffed with mushrooms, fresh garlic, the cold salads Nell brought last night and kettle corn. Betsey also had two cases of homemade root beer in her root cellar she made last summer. They had many different wines and Betsey would make homemade cocoa. Joshua had the fire going and they all moved into the living room to warm up.

The chatter was all about opening day events. Joshua would handle the sleigh rides, Alexis would cover the ice-skating, Betsey and Sahara would handle the entertaining, food, and drinks. The phone rang and Betsey went to answer it. She was shocked to hear warden Bob on the other end. Hi Bob what is wrong, is James ok, with fear in her voice. I am sorry to have to tell you James was in a confrontation with another inmate it was very serious.

Betsey gasped for air. Is James ok? Bob said James is banged up a bit and had some stitches, but would recover fine. Betsey did not want to ask about the other inmate. She took a deep breath and asked how the other inmate was. Bob hesitated and said it was not good. He was in intensive care at a local hospital. Betsey went into a state of shock. Bob was talking but she was barely hearing him. When Betsey heard James would go into solitary confinement and would have an added sentence of five more years if the man dies, Betsey dropped the phone and crumbled to the floor still trying to breath.

Joshua heard the loud thump and headed to Fourier were she had gone to answer the phone. Everyone else was right behind him. They found Betsey curled up in a ball and a man's voice asking if she was still there. Joshua picked up the receiver and began to speak, as the line went dead, no one was there. Sahara and Alexis got Betsey to her feet and sat her down on the couch in the living room. Joshua sat down beside her and took her in his arms while yelling for someone to get her a glass of brandy. She was shaking and white as a ghost. Sahara came with the glass of brandy and made her take a sip.

Sahara , so worried for Betsey if James was gone for good too; she would not be able to handle that right now after losing her parents last year. James was all she had.

The whole room was silent waiting for Betsey to recover from shock. As she sipped the brandy, her color was returning and she stopped shaking. Everyone's eyes were on her as she started to speak. She kept repeating she had to call Bob. Sahara gasped that is the warden at the prison! Sahara ran to Betsey's side and grabbed her hand. Its James, please tell us what is wrong.

Betsey took a deep breath, he was in a fight and it is not good as she wept. Sahara ran and got her some Kleenex. Betsey was able to compose herself and headed to the phone. Sahara told them to wait in the living room and she followed her to the Fourier. Betsey dialed the phone and heard Bob's voice at the other end. Bob please can I talk with James? Bob told her not tonight but would see what he could do in the morning. He told her he would be in touch tomorrow on updates regarding the situation that James would be facing. Betsey thanked him and hung up the phone, still tears in her eyes. Sahara hugged her and told her she was there for her.

Joshua knew what had happened and could not be more pleased! See, he had friends at the prison from an earlier sentence he had served years ago for a bar fight. Joshua had called in a favor from a man that owed him still serving a 20-year sentence there. He tried his best to seem upset and tried to console her. His plan to get rid of James was in motion now.

It was hard not to show how thrilled he was to their guests and Betsey. Their guests were getting ready to leave and let Betsey have some time alone, when Joshua stopped them and said they should stay. He went on to say Betsey needed her friends now more than ever. They decided he was right and all tried to cheer her up with talk about her big opening day. Betsey was able to smile, regarding her new venture at keeping the family farm. All was a buzz about how good this was for Betsey and the community.

It was late and Betsey was very tired after her upsetting

news earlier today. Their guests started to leave, as they were going they told Betsey that they would return early the next day to help in any way they could. Betsey began to cry and hugged them. She knew she would be all right as to having friends of the community to help her and the family farm. As Sahara hugged her, she told her she would stay the night if Betsey needed her. Betsey told her she would see her and Alexis in the morning. She told Sahara not to worry as Joshua would be with her and they said goodnight.

After they left the driveway he commanded Betsey to go to bed, he would clean up the kitchen. She did not fight him tonight and headed up to bed. Betsey washed up and got into bed. Joshua was in the kitchen dancing as he washed up dishes and glasses from their guests. He now could relax and settle in to Mainstay.

Betsey cried herself to sleep thinking about the wardens' phone call earlier. Joshua finished the dishes, poured himself a nightcap, and sat in the living room. It was midnight now and he himself was not tried, just excited about his future. He took the pink quartz ring from his pocket and thought on the best time to give it to Betsey. It would be soon things were going his way.

He finished his drink and headed up to bed. He entered the bedroom to find Betsey sleeping with Kleenex surrounding her face. He cleaned them up and gave her a kiss on the cheek. He wanted so much to make love to her, but thought not due to the circumstances earlier tonight.

He laid there for hours it seemed, watching her sleep as he planned their future together. He knew James would be out of that future, as his master plan was in motion.

He tried to get some sleep, as he knew morning would come soon.

Betsey awoke at five o'clock am screaming James name. Joshua jumped at her cries. He hugged her as she melted in his arms sobbing. He wiped her tears from her eyes and kissed her. She tried to pull away from him but could not. Before she could stop him, he was undressing her, creasing her breasts and kissing her neck. They ended up making passionate love, which ended in the shower.

As they dressed, Betsey was very distant and quiet. This worried him. He tried to start up a conversation about the big day. Betsey just headed down stairs to the kitchen.

There was much to accomplish yet for opening day. Her mind was spinning with the bad news given to her the night before. How could she ignore this and go on with the opening. She made herself a cup of coffee with a kicker in it to calm herself from yesterday's events. How could she have given into him knowing her husband was in trouble? How could she not go through with the opening? She knew now it was up to her to save the family's legacy.

CHAPTER 12

Her parents loved this farm more than life itself as well as her and James did. She needed to pull herself together and make this happen, she tried to pull herself together for the events of opening day. Betsey knew things were looking bad for her husband now and she had to accomplish saving the farm at all cost. As she was trying to convince herself of this venture, Joshua entered the kitchen and asked if she was ok. She was startled and said hi, yes, I am ok. She was lying to him. He could tell the news was upsetting her, and tried to talk about what he could do to help her for opening day today.

Betsey asked Joshua if he was hungry she would make him some breakfast. He said he would just have some coffee with what she was having. She let out a laugh and said if you are sure! She poured him a cup with brandy and refilled her own. Joshua took a sip and coughed as he smiled; guess I was not so good this morning! She told him she was still upset due to her husband's new situation. He asked {already knowing} what that might be. She explained to him about the fight and the condition of the inmate James had confronted. He listened with the anticipation of his plan paying off. Husband locked up for life and old cellmate perishing. How great was this turning out for him!

Betsey noticed the smirk on his face and was hurt at his reaction to the news. He quickly lost the smirk and told her he would help in any way he could to help her and James. There was a knock at the door and it startled them. It was only six thirty in the morning. Betsey headed to the door to find Sahara there. Betsey was thrilled to see her and gave her a hug. Sahara could tell she was taken back from the news on James. Sahara hugged her friend and told her everything would be fine.

Betsey invited her in and they went to the kitchen where Joshua was preparing breakfast. Sahara apologized for coming so early. Joshua said no problem; they had plenty of food for all and asked her to sit down at the kitchen table. Betsey got her a cup of her special coffee of the morning. Sahara took a sip and laughed. Betsey you still know how to surprise me! Joshua agreed and they all laughed.

He made French toast with butter and strawberries on top. In addition, some sausage links on the side. They sat and ate while going over today's events. Sahara was worried for her friend, yet another tragic happening in her life. Betsey was just starting to gain ground on her life. She and James's dreams were starting to come true and then this. She would try to guide her on not investing any more money on James. He apparently was not thinking of Betsey anymore. How could he after what he had done now!

Breakfast was done and people started to arrive at the farm, no time for thinking about James now. Things needed to revolve around the events of the day. It was a great turn out for their opening. Many attended from the community and visitors from surrounding states as well.

It was great weather for the events. The sun was shining and temperatures were comfortable.

Everyone enjoyed the events and food at the Inn that day. It was going on seven o'clock and the crowed was fading. Betsey's close friends were still there as the rest had left. As they sat in the house, Joshua started a fire in the fireplace to warm the house as temperatures were dropping out side. Betsey, Alexis and Joshua combined their money from the day's events in one bowel. They all sat in front of the fire and counted the profit of the day. Betsey jumped up and headed for the phone. She had forgotten to call for more information on James.

The phone rang several times before Bob answered. Bob, Betsey asked, how was James? Bob was silent for a moment then answered, he is recovering fine, and the inmate he fought with passed away this morning due to the stab wounds inflicted by James. Betsey dropped the phone and began to cry. Sahara and Nell were ease dropping on her call and came to grab her before she hit the floor. They both hugged her and told her they would help her through this.

Meanwhile Joshua appeared with a hand full of money. Honey we cleared five hundred dollars today. In addition, we booked two more couples for a stay at the Inn this fall. He knew what news she had gotten, but could not wait to tell her this news. Joshua also wanted to confirm the information he had received earlier today from another inmate he spent time with on his cellblock that things looked grim for James.

By the look on Betsey's face, he knew it was true. Betsey went through the story with him as he was thinking of how to give her the ring and not listening to her as she told him about James; he already knew the fate of her husband. Betsey was upset she could not talk with her husband.

Betsey knew she needed to call their lawyer Attorney Carlson and fill him in on the new charges against her husband. It would have to wait for morning now. All her friends from town were in the living room drinking and talking about the day's events. Betsey joined them and could not thank them all enough for the help and support. They told her not just today but would be there for her until she did not need them anymore. She was very emotional and thanked them with all her heart.

Betsey's husband was in a lot of trouble again and Betsey did not know what could have caused him to hurt another person, he had always been so gentle. What happened to her easygoing man? Who was he really? What she did not know was her houseguest Joshua was the cause of her new nightmares. He would and will do anything to keep her for himself.

Morning came early again for Betsey. Another night not much sleep, she woke at dawn again and took her shower, dressed and headed down stairs. Joshua was still asleep. He was feeling confident now, no worries.

Betsey went to the barn and took care of the horses. She sat out there for a while contemplating what to do next. She was numb and distraught at her new situation. How could her life get so complicated? Joshua alarmed her as he sat down next to her. He asked her what he could do to help to improve her mood as due to the circumstances of her husband's actions.

Making it all go away would be great right now, she replied. Betsey asked him if he could do magic? He smiled and said he thought he had! She was a little confused at that statement then smiled and blushed. Betsey looked at her watch it was nine o'clock, she could call the lawyer now. She took off running for the house and Joshua followed. They reached the house and Betsey headed for the phone. He stopped her and said thought you were racing me for more delight! She pushed him away and said she had business to take care of today.

Betsey dialed the number to their lawyer. The phone rang, rang, and rang but no answer. Betsey thought this was odd. Betsey was beside herself by no answers at Carlson's office. Joshua said he would go tend to the office for the hayrides scheduled for today. They were expecting a group on vacation for hayrides before heading home.

She turned the TV on for the morning news. To her disbelief it was showing how there had been a brutal murder in their community last night. The Carlson children had found James' lawyer and his wife dead at their home this morning. The children had returned for spring break from college. Betsey grabbed the phone and called the sheriff's office.

A deputy, Carl, whom she had gone to school with, answered the phone. Betsey asked for Sheriff Burk. Carl told her he was out at the Carlson's estate. Betsey let him know who she was and he said how sorry he was for her husbands' misfortune. Betsey quickly told him of the problem that accrued last night with James and how she tried to call their lawyer regarding the matter and had gotten no answer. Betsey continued to explain how she had seen the murders on the news. Carl told her he was so sorry and would have Sheriff Burk call her as soon as he returned to the station. Betsey thanked him and hung up the phone. She did not realize Joshua was standing behind her; she was startled by his presence.

He asked what was wrong and she began to tell him as the bell rang at the outside office. He left to attend to the bell. He knew what news she had received. His plan was still in motion! Betsey was so distracted by the news she did not even hear the service bell. What would this mean for her and James?

CHAPTER 13

Attorney Carlson knew the case that was against James and could have helped with his new trial. Betsey looked out the kitchen window getting lunch ready and realized their hayride group was there. Joshua was helping them up onto the wagon for their hayride. Betsey had totally forgotten about their booking for this morning. She needed to prepare a lunch for them, how could she have forgotten! Betsey hurried getting venison burgers ready for the grill along with a cold baby crescent salad. She would also add olive oil, sugar, ground black pepper, sea salt, baby shrimp and cucumbers. This needed to chill at least one hour. She should have prepared it this morning!

The news of Attorney Carlson and his wife had shaken her. Betsey had the salad made and in the refrigerator, chilling patties made for the grill and fresh rolls ready for lunch now. She was back on schedule, as soon as she heard the bell ring the ride would be over and she would then start the grill for lunch.

Betsey was preparing the table for lunch when the phone rang. She ran for the phone and grabbed the receiver to hear Sherriff Burk's voice on the other end. Betsey? Yes, this is Betsey. Hi, this is Sheriff Burk; you called earlier regarding Attorney Carlson. Yes I did, I was worried I could not reach him this morning. Then I heard on the news his wife and him were murdered. Their children had discovered them.

Sheriff Burk could only give her information that was already on the news. He said he was sorry but it was an ongoing murder case. Betsey thanked him for returning her call and hung up.

Betsey barely heard the cowbell that the hayride was over they would be up for lunch. She hurried out to the grill and lighted it for lunch. Betsey heard the doorbell ringing and ran to the front door. It was Sahara and Alexis. They gave Betsey a hug and told her how sorry they were about the news of the Carlson's. Betsey invited them in and ran for the deck; she had started the grill for lunch. Sahara and Alexis tried to keep up with Betsey as she was babbling about lunch for the guests!

They met up with her on the deck. They were glad at the business already for the farm. They were hoping this would take her mind off the murders and James. Joshua and the hayride party of six headed up on the deck. Betsey tried to smile and greet them. Joshua could tell she was coming unglued.

Betsey invited them into the house and said lunch would be ready soon. Sahara and Alexis took over and brought the guests in to the dining room to be seated for lunch. Joshua grabbed her in the kitchen and asked what was going on, although he already knew. She told him to wait until the guests had gone please! He grabbed the patties and headed out to the grill.

As Joshua was grilling, he was feeling good about the job he had done keeping James behind bars for years. It was only up from here for him! Joshua finished grilling the venison burgers and headed for the kitchen where

Betsey was taking her salad out of the refrigerator. She placed the burgers on the homemade buns and put them on a platter for the table. He took the platter and she took the salad to the dining room table for the guest's lunch.

They all sat down to lunch as Betsey told Sahara and Alexis she had plenty of food for all. Joshua was surprised to see them there! They all enjoyed the lunch, and the guests scheduled a one-week stay in July as well. Betsey was over come at the success already with Mainstay Inn. Sahara and Alexis helped her clean up after the guests had left.

Joshua headed out to put the wagon away in the barn. He was disturbed at how clinging Betsey's friends were with her. They had finished up in the kitchen and were waiting for Joshua to come back into the house. He was having a fit out in the barn. How could he have Betsey with all these people always dropping in? He tossed around hay and tools. Joshua then felt better. He headed for the house knowing Betsey's friends would still be there. He needed to get his emotions under control now.

He entered the house to hear them talking about his masterpiece, the murders of Attorney Carlson and his beloved wife. Joshua entered the living room were the girls were sitting. All turned their heads and said hi to him, giggling on how handsome he was. He loved their reaction to him. He knew they would always be his puppets!

They all sat and talked for a while about upcoming events at Mainstay Inn. Sahara and Alexis left around two that afternoon. Joshua already had a romantic night planned for Betsey and him. He was going to take her to dinner in town and a walk down at the waterfront again.

The first date went so well he wanted to repeat it. Therefore, they headed off to downtown Salem. They arrived at 5 pm. They stopped in to see Nell; she had closed for the day as she had attended the opening at Mainstay Inn. They entered the store thru the back door. Nell was giving out instructions for the next day's menu. Betsey said hi, hope we are not bothering you? We decided to come into town for the night with everything going on.

Nell told them to have a seat and would be with them soon. Joshua pulled out a chair for Betsey at a table near the window. She sat and looked out over the cove of Salem it was so peaceful.

Nell soon joined them and asked about the Carlson's murders. Betsey was very upset still regarding the news. Nell could tell and apologized for bringing it up. Nell went on about the Mainstay Inn; this seemed to lighten the mood of all. Joshua said how they were going to eat at India West Restaurant for dinner.

He asked if Nell wanted to join them for dinner. She said it sounded wonderful but she had too much to do for her restaurant for tomorrows meals. She thanked them for the invite and they headed to India West.

Betsey and Joshua arrived at India West; they ordered and enjoyed their food once again. After supper, they walked down to the waterfront as before. This time they ran into Todd and Samantha from Birmingham Market at the waterfront park. Samantha ran to give Betsey a hug and Todd shook Joshua's hand. They went on about the buzz of the farm. Samantha asked Betsey how she was doing, as James was in more trouble and all the news about James lawyer and wife murdered! How horrible was that.

Betsey agreed and asked if they had heard anymore about the case? They both said no and wanted to know how the Inn was doing. They were sorry they missed the party, as well as opening day. Betsey and Joshua filled them in on what had been going on. They were glad to inform them of the bookings for spring and summer. They were so pleased with the good news. Joshua said they needed to go, but for them to stop out to the farm.

As Betsey and Joshua were leaving the park, a carriage pulled up to the curb. The driver stopped and asked Betsey to get in. She looked back at Joshua and he followed her into the carriage. They pulled up to the gazebo at Community Park and Joshua got out and took her hand. He walked her into the gazebo and knelt down on one knee. Betsey surprised by it she tried to run away. He grabbed her back and took out the ring box from his pocket. Joshua opened the box and took her hand. Betsey was shocked it was the pink quartz ring she had previously seen in a storefront window. He took her hand and put it on her finger. She looked at him, grabbed him, and gave him a big kiss. He replied I was hoping you would feel this way!

Joshua told her how much he loved her and never wanted to be without her. Betsey blushed and gave the ring back to him. He looked confused by this. She was crying and said I am still married to James and could not except such a gift from another man. Joshua hugged her and said he knew but still wanted to give her something nice for what she has done for him. He went on to tell her the last couple of weeks had been the best time in his life.

Betsey cried even harder now at his comments. She took back the ring and put it on her finger. They got back on the carriage. When the ride was over they got off down on the waterfront near the boats. They walked holding hands along the shops talking to everyone they passed. They looked like newlyweds to all the people they passed.

It was getting late now and the wind was picking up so they headed back uptown to the truck to head home. On the ride home Betsey could not take her eyes off the ring. Joshua noticed and took her hand in his. The remainder of the trip home they held hands.

It was late when they had arrived home at 11: 00 pm. When they entered the house Betsey noticed the light blinking on the answering machine. She played the message. It was from Sherriff Burk. He needed to talk to her regarding the Carlson's murders. Joshua was very quiet after hearing the message. Why would he want to talk to Betsey? What could she know regarding the case? Betsey said it had been a long day and was heading up to bed. Joshua said he was going to sit up for a while and kissed her goodnight. Betsey fell sound asleep when her head had hit the pillow.

Downstairs Joshua was pacing the floor worrying about Sherriff Burk. In addition, what did he want to talk to Betsey about? He knew he had not left any evidence behind at the Carlson's, so he thought. Betsey had gone to bed before him that night. Did she awaken and know he was not there? How could he ask her without arousing suspicion? He was sure he left nothing behind to incriminate himself, he had been very careful.

On the way home, he buried all his clothes and the knife out in the woods 1 mile from the farm. Betsey had been sound asleep that night when he had gotten into bed. He was worrying for nothing and headed up to bed.

Joshua watched Betsey sleep for a while and knew how lucky he was to have her in his life. When Joshua awoke, Betsey was all ready out of bed. As he went downstairs to find her, he heard her talking on the phone. He sat on the step and listened to her conversation. She was talking to Sherriff Burk. All he was able to hear was her telling him she does not know anything about James' file. The file Joshua needed to get rid of yet! How stupid of him to have kept it.

Joshua went back up stairs and got into the shower, he needed to think of something to tell her why he had to go out this morning. He went downstairs and found Betsey in the kitchen making breakfast. He walked up behind her and gave her a hug and kiss.

They sat down to breakfast and Joshua told her he needed to go into town to have the oil changed in his truck and would be back soon. Betsey was still thinking about her phone call with Sherriff Burk and barely heard him. Joshua gave her a kiss goodbye and said he would not be long. Betsey said fine, see you later as she was preoccupied with James and the murders.

Betsey needed to talk to James and get his side of the story. She could no longer count on his lawyer anymore. Betsey went to the phone to call the prison to arrange a visit with James.

Warden Bob speaking how can I assist you? Hi, Bob

its Betsey Willard, James Willard's wife. Yes how are you Betsey, what can I do for you? I need to see James as soon as possible; we need to hire a new lawyer. Bob said how sorry he was about Attorney Carlson and his wife, it could not have happened at a worst time. Betsey said she was still in shock from the horrible news, all of it! He was sorry to inform her James was still in lock down, no visitor's, only legal counsel allowed.

Betsey began to cry, thanked him for his time, and then dropped to the floor. She was not sure how long she had laid there on the floor. She was startled by knocking at the front door. Betsey got up off the floor, wiped tears from her eyes, and opened the door. Sahara was standing there holding a basket of food Nell had sent for them to eat. Betsey invited her in and Sahara asked if she was ok, you look like hell!

Betsey started to sob and said no! She took the basket from Sahara and headed for the kitchen. Sahara followed her and sat down at the table. She asked were Joshua was? Betsey said he had to go into town for service on his truck.

Joshua was on his way into town but not before stopping at the spot where he had buried the murder weapon and bloody clothes. He picked them up and put them in garbage bags along with James file.

He was now heading for the north end of town were the cliffs looked over the bay of Salem. He would drive up the old logging road that is no longer used. This would bring him to a deserted area along the top of the cliffs. Joshua had stopped at the town library when he came to Salem to get familiar with the area. He knew this was a good spot to dump the bags. He could toss them into the rough currents at the bottom of the cliffs.

He drove thru town hoping not to be seen as he drove to the logging road. He turned onto the logging road looking around before driving up to the top. He was sure no one had seen him enter the road. At the top, he got out of the truck, looked around again and tossed the bags off the cliff. The bags had hit the water below and churned into the rough current below. He should stop and get his oil changed as to have a receipt showing he had.

Betsey was telling Sahara about James' new added sentence due to fighting with an inmate and killing him. Betsey needed to find a lawyer as quick as possible to help James. As they were looking in the phone book for a new lawyer for James, the phone rang.

Sahara went to answer the phone as Betsey was preoccupied with looking for a lawyer. It was Sheriff Burk asking to speak with Betsey. Sahara was telling him that the town was scared after the murders. Did he have any leads to the case? He informed her they had some, hopefully more by the end of the week. He told her not to worry as he thought it was an isolated incident.

Sahara called Betsey to the phone. Hi, Sheriff Burk how I can help you, she asked. He wanted to know if he could come out to the farm to talk with her this evening. She told him yes, she would be home all night. They agreed on 6:00 o'clock, he would join them for dinner also. Sherriff Burk had recently divorced and could use a home cooked meal.

As Betsey was finishing up with the Sherriff, Sahara found a new upcoming lawyer from in town. Apparently, he just moved here with his wife from New York City.

Attorney Thornton specialized in criminal law. Betsey grabbed the phone and called his office. She reached his answering machine and left a message. Betsey and Sahara headed back into the kitchen to open the basket of food from Nell. It contained gourmet wraps, homemade soups, a loaf of French bread, freshly baked with rosemary, and fresh pastries. Nell's generosity overcame Betsey as she put away the food.

Betsey was worried about Joshua; he should have been back by now! Joshua was on his way back to the farm, going over his tracks of the day. He knew he had covered himself and the thought to get his oil changed to have a receipt was genius.

Joshua was feeling quite good on how he handled anyone coming between him and Betsey. He knew Attorney Carlson was working on getting James released for a lesser sentence than five years. It had been in public records at the library that he filed for a new trial with the higher courts as self-defense case. James would have gotten a new trail. He had to stop Attorney Carlson; his wife just had gotten in the way. Joshua's mind started to wander to how lovely Mrs. Carlson had been. Her pearly white tight thighs and buttocks, making love to her felt almost as good as Betsey!

Too bad Mrs. Carlson did not think it was the best she had ever had! He was startled back to reality when his tires were hitting the edge of the road. Joshua turned his wheel as not to go off the road. He let out a laugh and continued on home singing to the radio.

CHAPTER 14

As Joshua drove up the driveway Sahara and Betsey were on the front porch. They both waved to him and he was glad to be home. Yes, this was his home now!

When he started up the steps of the porch, Joshua heard Betsey and Sahara talking about a new lawyer. His blood began to boil! How could she still be thinking about saving James? He was not the man for her; she needed a real man to take care of her! One that knew how to kill and get away with it! Betsey asked him if everything was ok. He looked a little nervous and said yes, why do you ask? She told him he had been gone a long time in town.

Joshua remembered he had stopped and picked up some flowers for her, he raced back to the truck to get them. Joshua came back up the steps with the flowers and Betsey forgot about him taking so long in town. She took the flowers from him and said goodbye to Sahara. Sahara giggled, and gave her and Joshua a hug before leaving. She then told Betsey she would give her a call tomorrow to check in on any new news regarding James and the Carlson's murders.

When Joshua and Betsey entered the house, he asked her what she and Sahara had been talking about on the porch. He had a hard time controlling his temper after hearing what they had been discussing. Betsey started to fill him in on the day's news as she headed for the kitchen. Joshua's blood was boiling the more he heard. When Betsey told him Sheriff Burk would be joining them for dinner he lost it!

He took several deep breaths before asking Betsey why he would be joining them for dinner. Betsey laughed and told him not to worry about their relationship, as Sherriff Burk was not old friends with her or James. She continued to tell him the Sheriff had moved here two years ago from Chicago. He was not going to judge them for the way they were living. He only wanted to talk with her, as Attorney Carlson had been James' lawyer during his trail.

Joshua was feeling uncomfortable having to dine with a cop, knowing he was an ex prisoner and he had murdered the Carlson's. Betsey asked him if he was feeling ok, as the color had gone white in his face. He replied, no I am feeling a little flushed. I think I should go lie down, sorry about dinner. I will meet Sheriff Burk another time.

Betsey was disappointed he would not be joining them for dinner; she understood and said she would bring him some soup and bread later. Joshua thanked her and headed up to bed. Betsey set the dining room table for dinner and heated up the chicken gumbo soup Nell had sent for dinner. She would also serve the buffalo chicken wraps. She would heat up left over chicken soup and bread for Joshua.

Joshua went up stairs got undressed and laid in bed, his mind reeling on if he was sure he covered himself, due to the crimes he had committed. He felt confident he should be absent from the night visit with Sheriff Burk. It was 5:30pm and Betsey headed up stairs with soup and hot bread for Joshua. He heard her coming, covered up with the blanket as if he was cold, and turned off the bedroom light.

Betsey entered the room and turned on the light, Joshua I have some supper for you. He slowly raised his head from the covers and said Betsey you are too good to me! She laughed and asked how he was feeling. He told her much better being in bed but wished she could join him though. Betsey told him, still horney even sick!

Betsey set the tray down on the bed and fluffed up the pillows behind his head. She made him sit up and set the tray in front of him. Betsey started spooning soup in his mouth for him. Joshua felt bad for his part of lying about being sick! He never had anyone take care of him when he was sick, not even his own mother! Joshua told her he felt fine and just needed some sleep. Betsey made sure he finished his soup, then headed down stairs.

As she reached the bottom step the doorbell rang; it startled her almost dropping the tray. Betsey set the tray down on the entry table at the front door and opened the door. It was Sheriff Burk. Betsey invited him in to the living room and went back to get the tray. Sheriff Burk noticed she had a tray of empty dishes. You have company staying in the house he asked. Betsey said yes and headed for the kitchen asking what he would like to drink. He followed her to the kitchen and said a beer would be fine. Betsey set the tray down on the counter and opened the refrigerator to get a bottle of beer.

Joshua had gotten out of bed and sat at the top of the stairs to listen to what they were talking about. Betsey found a bottle of beer in the back of the refrigerator that use to be James. She took it out and gave it to Sheriff Burk. Betsey then poured herself a glass of wine and headed back into the living room. Sheriff Burk followed her and they both sat down on the couch. Betsey started the conversation by saying glad to have you out to the farm. Do you have any new news regarding the case? He told her no, but hoped she could help.

Betsey asked how she could possibly help. Sheriff Burk said James' file was the only one missing from the file cabinets. That made him look at her or James for answers. Betsey felt horrified that their murders could have been because of her and James. How could this be happening to them! Sheriff Burk could tell this was upsetting her and making Betsey very uncomfortable.

Betsey began to tell him about what had occurred at the prison and how much trouble James was in, due to the fight and the outcome of it with the inmates' death. Joshua was pounding his fist into his legs at what Betsey was bringing up to Sheriff Burk. He would check into the prison and eventually his name would pop up on the radar, as he was an ex-convict for assault as well sexual assault. He needed to keep a low profile now.

Sheriff Burk showed Betsey pictures taken at the scène of the Carlson's murders. Joshua sat at the top of the stairs and relived the photos. Betsey had seen the horrible things that happened to them. Attorney Carlson stabbed several times before dying. The count was 26 times but they say he died at 10. Mrs. Carlson, who was raped three times or more, vaginal and anal scaring, and stabbed at least 20 times, there were teeth marks in her breast for god's sake! Betsey threw the pictures and ran to the bathroom to vomit.

Sheriff Burk hated to show her those pictures but needed to for information she may have that could help the case. Betsey returned and Joshua wanted to kill the Sheriff. How dare he hurt Betsey this way!

Sheriff Burk apologized to her for having to have her view the pictures. He continued to tell her they thought James' trial could be the reason. Betsey, so confused at this, collapsed on the couch. Sheriff Burk went to her and tried to revive her. Betsey started to cough and was alert. Joshua was heading down stairs now to help Betsey. He did not care for his own safety now.

Joshua entered the room but did not surprise Sheriff Burk, hi Mr. Tripp, nice to meet you. I have heard a lot about you around town. Joshua extended his hand to him and shook his hand. Betsey blushed and told Sheriff Burk he was there helping run the farm while James was away. Sheriff Burk just smiled and said nice to meet you.

Betsey invited them into the dining room for supper. She went to the kitchen to get the soup and chicken wraps. Joshua excused himself to go take care of the horses. Betsey and Sheriff Burk sat down to Nell's food in the dining room as Joshua headed to the barn. Sheriff Burk went on to ask Betsey if she had talked with Attorney Carlson recently. As they ate, she told him she had not. Betsey went on to tell him what had happened to James in prison. He was sure this could be connected to the case of the Carlson's murders.

Betsey asked why he thought this. He went on to tell her that James' file was the only one missing. Betsey said he handled many criminal cases. How did they know it was because of James' case this happened, as his file was the only one missing. He went on to tell Betsey evidence found at the scene looked that way. Betsey was shocked at this news! She continued to tell him she was looking to hire a new lawyer for her husband.

She knew James was not guilty of the first murder and definitely not of the second murder. He asked her about Joshua Trip. He is a farmhand, which my best friend recommended. He has been nothing but helpful and caring! Betsey did not want any more questions; she was sick and tired after seeing the pictures. Betsey told him all she knew and asked him to leave.

Sheriff Burk could see how upset Betsey was and left the farm for now. His investigation was far from over at the farm. He had a gut feeling the answers lay here at Mainstay Inn. As his SUV drove out of the driveway, Joshua returned to the house from the barn.

Betsey was in the kitchen washing glasses and plates from dinner. Joshua came up behind her and hugged her also kissing her neck. He began caressing her breasts. Betsey was putty in his hands! He grabbed her in his arms and carried her up stairs to bed where he had his way with her.

Joshua laid her on the bed and tore her clothes off. Betsey quivered with excitement! He was forceful yet gentle. He ravished her thighs and buttock, which drove her to madness! Then he worked his way up to her breasts. Betsey was in a trance. As they indulged in each other, organisms were strong and hard for both. Their bodies moved as wild animals did making love. After hours of wild passion, they ended in each other's arms. Sweaty and exhausted, Betsey said, for a sick man you are ok in my book and laughed.

Joshua drew her closer and said I love you Betsey girl! Please remember that! I would do anything for you. What Betsey did not know was Joshua thought he already had in his mind.

CHAPTER 15

Sleep came easy for both their bodies were exhausted. They needed to get up early; some local kids and their parents were coming for horseback riding lessons. The alarm went off at six o'clock sharp. They got up, took their showers and headed down for breakfast. Joshua thought this would be a good time to ask Betsey about her visit with Sheriff Burk. Betsey said she did not want to talk about it, she would rather forget it. This made him feel uncomfortable and angry. How could she shut him out like this!

They sat and ate in silence, which was increasing Joshua's anger. He was thinking, "You bitch" how ungrateful. As Betsey started to clean up from breakfast, Joshua grabbed her hand and demanded she tell him what was going on. Betsey was shocked and tried to pull her hand away. She told him that she was feeling stressed, and they had a busy day ahead of them, maybe later. He could see she was upset about something and her face looked drawn. Therefore, he would wait for her to tell him later.

Joshua headed to the barn to feed and water the horses and get the saddles, bridles and blankets ready for the lessons for today. Betsey cleaned up the dishes and started to prepare food for lunch. After lessons, the guests get lunch with lessons. It had been a special they offered to get business. So far it had been working.

Betsey was preparing a fresh bowel of fruit, cut up and sugared. She would have hotdogs for the kids and buffalo burgers for the parents. Betsey had her rosemary rolls baking in the oven for the guests. She had plenty of water crescent and spinach salad that Nell had sent to serve as well.

Joshua was waxing the saddles, bridles and thinking about what Sheriff Burk was grilling Betsey about regarding the case. He still was very angry with her for pushing him away. He knew he had to hold his temper to keep her. Betsey had finished up in the kitchen; rolls just came out of the oven and were cooling on a rack. She headed to the barn to see if Joshua needed any help. As she was leaving the house, the phone rang. Betsey went to answer it.

It was Attorney Thornton's secretary asking her if she could come in today to speak with him. Betsey was so torn; she needed to be at the farm but could make it by four o'clock, if that was all right with her. The appointment was set for four o'clock today. Betsey had a big relief knowing she would get some help for James.

She started to head for the barn again as Joshua came through the kitchen door. Hi, she said, was just heading out to see if you needed some help. Joshua noticed the change in her face and attitude. No babe, everything is under control, but thank you. She began to tell him she needed to go into town at four o'clock to see a new lawyer for James. Joshua had all he could do to keep a smile on his face."What do you mean", he asked! Sahara and I found him in the phone book yesterday. I am hoping he can help James, she replied.

Joshua sat her down and informed her James killed two men in cold blood. Betsey pulled away and yelled self-defense! Before he could say anymore, the bell rang at the service building. He told her they would talk about this later, he had to go. Betsey was dancing around the kitchen getting things ready for lunch. She hopes that now she could help James.

Betsey remembered to call Sahara to update her on her visit with Sheriff Burk and Attorney Thornton. Alexis had answered the phone and called her mother to the phone. Betsey started telling her that she was seeing Attorney Thornton at four. Moreover, how Sheriff Burk thought the murders had something to do with them.

Sahara gasped and asked how that could be possible? Betsey continued to explain how James' file was the only one missing at Attorney Carlson's home. Sahara was shocked and asked her if she wanted her to go with her to see the lawyer? Betsey thanked her, but said she needed to do this on her own right now. She hung up with Sahara not feeling well about this situation.

Alexis could see something was wrong with her mom. She asked what was wrong. Sahara told her daughter there was nothing for her to be worried about, Aunt Betsey would be fine.

Joshua had everyone having fun learning how to ride. He had a knack for making people feel comfortable. Betsey was out on the deck watching him work. He was amazing with what how he handled horses and people. She was so lucky to have him. If not for Joshua, the farm would be on the market for sale. Betsey knew it was hard for Joshua to hear her talk about her husband James. She and Joshua were getting so close as friends and lovers. He should know she still loved James very much, how could he not know her and who she was.

The lessons were ending so Betsey got the grill going for lunch. She had been so busy daydreaming she forgot to get out the condiments and set the tables on the deck for lunch. Just as Betsey was finishing up, the guests were heading up to the deck for lunch. Joshua was laughing and enjoying one of the child's mothers' company. They all sat down, Betsey brought out the food for Joshua to cook. Then she returned to the kitchen to get the rest of the food for lunch.

As she returned to the deck, she noticed Barbie flirting with Joshua at the grill. Barbie was recently divorced from her husband, a doctor in town, and was on the prowl. Well she was sniffing up the wrong tree here! Her and her ex had two children whom she only spent time with when they were home from private school in New Hampshire.

Barbie was more the cougar type. She would jump anything 10 years younger than she was. Betsey went over to the grill and tried to break them up. Joshua could see this was bothering Betsey and grabbed her, hugged and kissed her on the check. He continued that he was nothing without her by his side. Barbie took the hint and went to sit with her children. Betsey was blushing, and winked at Joshua.

Lunch went on without a hitch. All were full and so happy with their visit to the farm that they scheduled another lesson for next week. Betsey and Joshua waved goodbye as they all left. How wonderful it was, already a rebooking at the farm! Joshua headed to the barn to put away the saddles, bridles and blankets from today's lessons.

Betsey went to clean up the deck from lunch. Betsey was getting anxious to meet with Attorney Thornton. She finished cleaning and sat down for a cold glass of ice tea. Betsey had one hour until she had to leave for town. Joshua came up to join her on the deck for a glass of ice tea. It was 50 degrees out today with plenty of sun. What a great spring day.

Joshua told Betsey he was planning to take her into town for dinner anyway, so he could drop her off at the lawyers and pick her up after he did some shopping in town. Betsey thought that would be great and asked where they were going to eat. Joshua said to let him worry about that, just dress casual.

Betsey ran up stairs to change as Joshua did the same. They fought up the stairs to see who would reach the bedroom first. Betsey won, and hit the bathroom first. Joshua lay on the bed waiting for the bathroom planning his romantic night with Betsey. He really needed to "woo" her so she would give him the information he needed about James and the case.

He needed time in town to plan just that! His first stop would be Nell's; she could supply the food. Next would be the paper goods store, he would need plates and napkins, silverware, champagne glasses and a tablecloth. Next, he would have to get candles and holders. These maybe he could borrow from Nell. As they drove into town, both did not talk much. They reached town and Betsey told Joshua were to go. He dropped her off up town at the lawyer's office and said he would be back in an hour. As Joshua drove off Betsey smiled and entered the front door of the most gorgeous Victorian house. She had a feeling their luck was going to change.

When she entered the front hallway, she was breathless at the architect of the woodwork and wall panels. Betsey entered the office and saw a beautiful woman sitting behind this huge marble desk. She asked if she could help. Betsey replied I have an appointment with Attorney Thornton. Hi, Mrs. Willard, I am Nicky, have a seat and John will be right with you. Betsey sat and took in how beautiful the woodwork and ceilings were. Mr. Thornton had good taste.

Attorney Thornton's door opened and he and Sheriff Burk came out. "Hi, Betsey, nice too meet you again," said Sheriff Burk. Attorney Thornton introduced himself to Betsey and invited her in to his office. Please sit down Mrs. Willard. Betsey took a seat across from his desk in a charming velvet high back chair. Attorney Thornton asked her how he could help. Betsey began from the beginning of James' trouble. As she finished she asked if he could help them.

He told her they defiantly had a chance for a new trail regarding the circumstances of the charges against him. They both seemed cut and dry, self-defenses. Betsey was thrilled and could not thank him enough. He did go on to tell her the Carlson murders seem to be connected to James. As James' file was the only one missing. This shows someone was trying to cover-up the real evidence so that self-defense was not an option during a new trail. We have found out Attorney Carlson was working for the Russian mob as well.

They handle the fishermen's union in the states! Come to find out your husband's boat was under that union.

Betsey I know this is a lot for you to take in right now, but did James ever mention any problems at work? No Betsey replied. Please help him, he did not commit these crimes on his own, without it not being self-defense.

At the prison, they will not let me see him or talk to him. Attorney Thornton assured her he would go and see James tonight and file papers for a miss trial on both counts of murder. Betsey shook his hand and cried with relief. He felt her pain for her husband and assured her he would do the best he could to get James sentences reduced to a minimum. Betsey could not thank him enough for taking the case, especially after the Carlson's murders. He reassured her that Sheriff Burk and the department were closing in on the perpetrator involved in the murders. Betsey thanked him again and asked if he could give James a message for her? He said yes. Betsey told him to tell James she loved him very much and believed in his innocence always. Attorney Thornton, touched by this, promised that would be the first thing he told James.

Chapter 16

Betsey felt such relief knowing her husband had a great attorney to look out for his interests; she could breathe normal again. As she was leaving the office, she saw a memorial that was going to be held for Attorney Carlson and his wife at the town square tonight at six o'clock. Betsey really wanted to attend the memorial but did not know Joshua's plans.

Joshua was finishing their dinner plans. He had everything packed in the back of his truck ready for a dinner on the beach in the middle of March! As he pulled up to the curb were Betsey was waiting he thought, how did I get so lucky? Nell and one of her waiters had headed down to the south shore and decorated a grapevine terrace on the beach with white moon shaped lights and lavender garland. They also set a small table underneath it for their dinner. It was the most beautiful spot overlooking the bay.

Betsey got into the truck and told him about the Memorial services planned for this evening. It was already 5:30 now and the food was hot. He told her he felt bad but dinner could not wait. Betsey asked, could we not get later reservations? Joshua without spoiling the surprise said he would drop her off at the square and take care of their dinner seating and would be back.

He raced across town to Nell's to ask if they could keep the food warm, so Betsey could attend the memorial. As he approached the door, Nell was just locking up for the night. Joshua pleaded with her and she agreed to keep the food for one more hour. She knew how important this memorial was for Betsey. That is the only reason she agreed to it. Joshua promised he would be back in less than an hour and kissed Nell on the check to thank her. Nell could understand now how Betsey could be so taken by him.

Joshua left and headed up town to the square. He was able to leave his truck at Nell's and walk up to the square. Joshua spotted Betsey standing at the Carlson's memorial. He walked up to her and took her hand. She smiled and thanked him for changing their dinner reservation. He smiled and told her anything for her. Joshua did not want to be there, but not to look guilty stayed and talked with the people in town with Betsey. He did not want to let her in on the surprise dinner as they had to walk back to Nell's were he left his truck.

Betsey and Joshua were walking towards the south end of town and Betsey asked where they were going. As they approached Nell's, Betsey saw his truck parked in front. She asked, you had to park this far back here? Joshua just laughed and told her to wait in the truck; he would not be long. He went around back as planned earlier to get the food. Nell was sitting out back on the patio waiting for him. She got up and went in the back door to get his food. Joshua followed her and helped her carry the food. He thanked her again and carried the food to the truck. Joshua opened the back of the truck and set the food in the back.

As he got into the front seat, Betsey asked where he had gone. She could see Nell's was closed and in darkness. He just laughed and headed toward the South bay. He reached close enough to the spot where they would be dinning, pulled the truck over, and parked. He got out and went over to open Betsey's door. She got out of the truck and he led her to the beach. There was the lighted grapevine terrace with a table all set with linens and silverware and glasses. Joshua took her hand and led her to her seat. He told Betsey he would be right back.

Joshua ran to the truck and grabbed the food. When he returned she was sitting there with the moon light shining on her face; she was so beautiful. He nearly dropped the food! He set her plate of food down in front of her and she was amazed how he had pulled this off. It was roasted duck in cherry sauce. Betsey's favorite! Joshua poured the champagne and lighted the candles before sitting down.

Betsey, overwhelmed by all this began to cry. Joshua thought he had done something wrong. She got up, sat in his lap, and gave him a big kiss. I could not love you more than I do right now, she replied. They enjoyed their meal and sat for hours while looking at the bay. It was really getting cold now, time to pack up the truck and head home. One last stop at Nell's place. Joshua had to leave the table, linens, and candles on the back patio at Nell's place. Betsey laughed, I knew she had to be involved! She helped unload the truck with Joshua and then they headed home.

They reached home at midnight and were tired and cold. As soon as they got into the house, they headed to bed. It did not take long for them to fall asleep, as it had been a long day.

Joshua awoke first and headed down to the kitchen to put a pot of coffee on. He then headed to the shower and out to the barn to take care of the horses. Betsey was still asleep. She awoke to the smell of cinnamon coffee. Betsey got up and headed into the shower. After dressing, she went down stairs and poured a cup of coffee thinking about how Attorney Thornton and James were getting along. She could not wait to hear from the Attorney Thornton!

Joshua came thru the back door, poured himself a cup of coffee and sat down with Betsey. He asked how are you my love? Betsey smiled and said a little distracted. Betsey told him she was wondering how James and Attorney Thornton had made out with their first meeting. She was waiting for the attorney to call her.

Joshua got up and poured her another cup of coffee and started breakfast. Betsey went to help and he told her it was his turn to cook. He started with butter in a cast-iron pan then added two slices of rosemary bread to brown on each side. Joshua then cut small holes in the middle of each slice. He then dropped eggs into the holes and covered to continue cooking the eggs. Betsey remarked on how good it smelt. Joshua also had a couple of strips of smoked bacon sizzling in a pan.

They sat and ate breakfast over conversation regarding James and the murders. Betsey had promised him the day before to talk about the subjects. Betsey filled him in on her visit with Sheriff Burk also Attorney Thornton. Joshua sat and listened to what Betsey was saying but knew this was going to lead to him to being a suspect in the case by Sheriff Burk. He was feeling a little paranoid! He had committed the murders, his past, and he was new in town.

CHAPTER 17

Joshua was counting on his new name and identity as Joshua Tripp to keep him under the radar. He had acquired this name two months ago after getting out of prison. He was on the road walking by a farm in Tennessee.

John Black was tired and hungry. Joshua, then John Black, walked up the long driveway to a ranch a mile off the main road. He saw a beautiful girl sitting on the front porch. Horses were running out in the pastures. Joshua, then John Black, approached the girl and asked if he could have a cold drink? His presence startled her!

Her name was Mrs. Heidi Tripp. He introduced himself as John Black. Heidi invited him to sit down and poured him some iced tea she had made. John Black sipped the iced tea while asking about her about the ranch. Heidi told him her husband was out purchasing another horse for the farm, but would be home soon. She asked where he was from.

John Black told her he had been drifting for a while now but he was from Texas originally. He told her he had heard the horses and had missed home. Heidi laughed and said, "Nothing like it, the whining of horses will make you feel at home anytime". They sat and talked for an hour.

Then Joshua saw a truck with a trailer behind heading

up the long driveway. It was Heidi's husband Joshua Tripp. He got out of the truck and headed for Heidi to give her a hug and kiss. He noticed John Black sitting on his porch and introduced himself. Hi, I am Joshua Tripp, Heidi's husband, and you are? John told him the same story he had told Heidi. Then Joshua asked John what his plans were. John said he was just drifting for now was not sure.

Joshua told John he could use some help around the ranch if he was interested. John jumped at the offer as John did not know where he was heading at this point. It had been agreed that he stay in the quarters in the barn and help with the training of the horses. John would get room and board as well as meals and John would receive a salary along with the offer.

John Black was very pleased with the offer and agreed. Joshua showed John his living quarters after John helped him unload the new filly from the trailer to the pasture. He was an amazing white stallion. He had pride and stamina as well.

John had never seen an animal as gorgeous as him. Joshua told John they named the stallion Fireball. John thought that was a perfect name. Fireball had spirit, energy and beauty. He was unbelievable to watch! His spirit was raw and untamable. He owned his surroundings. Fireballs' mane and muscle structure were amazing, beauty in flight.

John wanted this kind of power and beauty in his life, he needed it. He craved it.

After releasing Fireball in to the pasture, Joshua brought John to the barn and the tack room where he would stay. John was thrilled at his new quarters! Prison only offered a small cell. Here he had a real bed, a desk and a bookcase with many books to read. In addition, a small bathroom to himself off his bedroom. After he had settled in, Joshua invited John up to the house for drinks and dinner. John thanked Joshua and said he would be up soon.

Joshua then headed for the house to his beautiful wife Heidi. He always missed her when he traveled. Heidi was working with the staff to prepare extra for their new guest for dinner. After this was accomplished, Heidi went to dress for dinner and her husband.

Her husband had been gone for a week now and she missed him every day he was gone. They all sat down to dinner in the dining room of the Tripp farm. John Black had felt right at home at the Tripp farm already.

Joshua and Heidi were very friendly and trusting folk. John knew this would be like taking candy from a baby! They sat and ate dinner over farm related conversation. The Tripp's were impressed on how much John Black knew about horse farms and horses.

Dinner was over and Joshua and Heidi were glad John would be staying on the farm as part of their team. John was thrilled; he had planned on it anyway!

John said he was tired so he would turn in for the night. Joshua walked him to the stables to John's room in the back of the stables. John Black said he could be very comfortable here. Joshua made sure John had been settled in to his new quarters and then headed back up to the house were Heidi was waiting for him in a red bustier.

She had missed Joshua when he was gone buying a horse for the ranch. Joshua picked her up and carried her to their bedroom upstairs. Joshua could not wait to get his wife undressed as he too had missed his wife as well. They had made passionate love, which seemed to last for hours as John watched them from the grounds under their bedroom window.

Morning came quickly for John but the excitement he had felt watching the Tripps make love was still on his mind. John said to himself that would be him making love to the beautiful Heidi soon! However, he would make her scream! Joshua and Heidi were up in the kitchen making breakfast when John knocked at the back door. They invited him in for breakfast. What they did not know was the devil had entered their home.

John and Joshua sat at the kitchen table having coffee as Heidi cooked breakfast talking about the horse Fireball that Joshua had brought home yesterday. John was telling them that Fireball was the most impressive horse he had ever laid his eyes on. Joshua had felt the same, which is why he had driven a long way to buy him. Joshua knew he could work with him to be a champion.

As breakfast ended, Joshua and John headed to the barn for a day's work on his ranch. When they arrived at the barn, the farmhands were already there ready for work. Butch and Tom were checking out the new horse, Fireball. Joshua introduced John to Butch and Tom who had worked for them going on 15 years now. John was thinking this could make his job a bit harder now!

They all went to work feeding, watering, getting clean hay and cleaning the stalls, twenty in all. When this was done they all headed to the corral were Fireball was being kept. Joshua had brought out the training bridle and rope to start with the breaking in of Fireball.

Joshua was impressed with Fireball as he walked him

around the corral. John, Butch and Tom were watching him work Fireball when Heidi arrived with ice tea and homemade cookies. They all took part in ice tea and cookies. Joshua started to head back into the corral with Fireball and invited John to join him. John was thrilled and accepted his offer. John felt a little out of his environment but took action, as if it had been yesterday he had broken a horse.

Fireball seemed to respect John and they danced as if partners! All were impressed with the instant bond Fireball had with John. Joshua was thinking he had found a perfect farmhand to work with the horses on their ranch. John really had a way with horses. His ability sure showed with Fireball.

Joshua and John worked with Fireball for hours and now it was time for trying to lay the blanket atop his back as to break him for riding. It did not go as easily as they thought! Fireball kicked and threw off the blanket many times. Heidi was ringing the bell at the house. This meant it was lunchtime. All headed up to the house for lunch.

Buffalo burgers and coleslaw were waiting for them on the back porch. Heidi also had fresh made ice tea awaiting them as well. As they ate, conversation was about Fireball. Butch and Tom told Joshua this was the most spirited horse he had brought home yet. This horse, they said, has a mind of its own. They both said he had a spirit like no other horse they had met. John knew this as well as he first noticed his eyes filled with white light!

John could not wait to get back to working with Fireball. Fireball and him were connected, this he knew. They were both unbroken and wild. They both shared passion at a higher level than most. John knew he would never be able to part with this horse.

Lunch was over and time to get back to work breaking Fireball. Joshua was impressed. In one hour, John was able to stay on Fireballs' back. Then Joshua tried to ride him. Fireball bucked him off several times. He gave up and handed the reins to John. John asked him to open the corral gate and him and Fireball took the ride of their lives. The feeling of pure thunder and muscle under John's legs made him want Heidi even more.

As he rode Fireball back to the corral, Butch and Tom were watching in disbelief. John cooled Fireball down, took the bridle and blanket off him, and brought him to the watering station. Joshua shook John's hand and told him he had never seen anything like it before.

Butch and Tom were washing the other horses in amazement on how John was so great around horses. They laughed saying he must be a horse whisperer! The day was ending and time for fun. Joshua and Heidi were planning a trip into town to the local saloon. They invited John to join them. Butch and Toms' wives would also be going. It would be a good chance to meet the town folk. John was happy with this invite. He needed to know what might be in his way of taking over the Tripp's. John was pleased to accept their offer.

John Black headed to his quarters to dress for the night out. Butch and Tom had headed home to do the same and to get their wives. All arrived at Nick's Saloon at six o'clock. They all sat at the big round table in the back room. They ordered barbeque spareribs and the best homemade coleslaw in the state. The server was new to them. Her name was Claudia from Orlando Fla. She had only worked there now for three weeks. Claudia knew the whole menu and specialty drinks already. She brought their food and rounds of pitchers of beer for their table. As they ate, they asked John how the ribs compared to Texas ribs. John said the barbeque sauce was the best here at Nicks as well as the ribs. He needed to know what was in the sauce!

John also knew he would get that, as the server seemed to have a crush on him as well as him with her; she was hot! Claudia returned to see if they needed anything else. John said yes. My achy bra - key heart needs a dance with you! Claudia laughed and said she would be off the time clock in one hour. John told her he would wait then for that dance.

Everyone else at the table laughed and said way to go dude. John loved it, fitting in and getting a piece of ass tonight as well!

He sat and watched Heidi and Joshua dance. He was jealous! The way they moved together on the dance floor and in the bedroom was amazing. John wanted that! He loved beautiful women. Moreover, especially those who could cook as well. Joshua and Heidi returned to the table and John asked Heidi to dance? She looked at her husband and he said "go-ahead sweetheart if you like". Therefore, John and Heidi hit the dance floor. John gave her the dance of her life. Heidi had to cool down afterwards outside.

John was hot and very romantic! Heidi was feeling guilty of the feelings she was having for another man on the dance floor. His eyes and his body movements against her body were hot! Heidi was taken with him. She told herself it must only be because of her husband being gone so much with his work that she craved another man's body contact.

Claudia returned to the table dressed for a night of romance. John was impressed how beautiful she looked. Claudia was a cowboys dream. She was no older than eighteen, which attracted him very much so. Claudias long tan legs, firm tight ass and perky breasts attracted him right off. John asked Claudia to dance. She accepted and they started for the dance floor when Joshua asked him were Heidi was? John said he did not know, after they finished their dance she headed towards the door.

Joshua went outside to look for her. He found her sitting on a rock smoking out front. Joshua approached Heidi and asked what was wrong? She put out the cigarette and her face was blushed. Heidi went on to tell Joshua how much she missed him when he was away, which was a lot lately. Heidi did not know when Joshua would leave again. She continued to tell him how lonely she had been. He promised her he would be around for a long while now.

Joshua told her how Fireball would bring them a big payoff. They could even think about traveling now for some fun. Heidi jumped up on him and hugged him saying you are the best. They walked back inside holding hands. John noticed this and got angry! He grabbed Claudia back to the table. As John and Claudia returned to the table, Joshua was telling Butch and Tom they could have the vacation they always wanted. He and Heidi would be leaving for a while to travel. John was shocked at this, yet thrilled too.

No one would be looking for the Tripps. John was so excited he invited Claudia out to the farm. What she did not know was she would never make it there!

Chapter 18

They left to drive out to the farm. When John had told Joshua his plans, Joshua told him to take his truck. He and Heidi would catch a ride with Burk and his wife. Burk lived the closest to the Tripps. So John grabbed Joshua's keys to the truck and took Claudia by the hand and led her to the truck. She did not know what John had in mind for her.

John and Claudia got into the truck and headed towards the ranch. As they drove, Claudia asked John how long he would be around. John thought "what a whore", will sleep with me tonight, but does not even know me. John had remembered a turn on the way to Nicky's place. It had looked secluded and private. He pulled off the main road onto this road. They drove awhile and Claudia asked him "Where are we going? This is not the way to the Tripp ranch". John just smiled and said, "I cannot wait to get you back to the ranch so I thought we would stop here first". She was feeling the same way and started to take off her blouse.

Claudia's breasts were gleaming in the moon light coming in thru the truck window. They were the best thing he had seen in a long time.

John was just released from prison where he had served a long time for assault charges. Seeing her pearly white plump perky breasts caused him to drive off the road. She continued to undress to her panties. Claudia's abs were so tight, and glistening in the moon light; it was driving John wild! He took her right then and there in the front seat of the truck. Then he dragged her outside and on to the ground. John pulled his pants off and jumped on top of her. He tore her panties off and threshed himself inside her.

Claudia moaned and moved underneath him. John grabbed her and turned Claudia over, she fought him, as she did not do it that way! He forced her head down in the dirt and had his way with her. Claudia tried to scream but ate dirt. She was in so much pain she blacked out. When John was thru with her he strangled Claudia and left her body lying there. He left her face down naked in the dirt. John got dressed and said," that's were pigs belong, in the dirt". John got back in the truck and drove back to the ranch.

John had parked the truck in front of the house and walked to the barn. Joshua and Heidi were not home yet. John took a shower and went to bed. Joshua and Heidi were awakened at six-o'clock am that morning to loud knocking at the front door. Joshua went to answer the door. It was Sheriffs Barnes at the front door with Deputy Clark. Sorry, to have woken you and Heidi, but Claudia from Nick's Place had been found raped and murdered this morning by tourists that had gotten lost off the main road. We were informed your farmhand John left the bar with her last night. Can we speak with him? Joshua told him "no problem, I will take you to him".

As they came close to the barn, John skipped out back to the corral where Fireball was. They knocked on John's door, but no answer. Joshua went to the house to get the key to open the door. Meanwhile, John was saddling up Fireball for a ride. He finished, mounted her and took off to the north fields. John could use Fireball as a reason he headed home alone to get some sleep. John would tell them he needed to be up early to train Fireball in the morning. Which he knew Joshua would confirm.

Joshua returned with the key and opened the door. Sheriff and Deputy Clark entered the room. John was not there! Joshua began to worry. Where was John? The Sheriff asked if they could search the room. Joshua knew his truck was back when he and Heidi got home.

How stupid could John have been! Using the Tripps' truck and leaving with Claudia. John ran Fireball hard as to make him sweat, to look as if he had been riding for hours. He sat upon him and thought what he would say. As John was heading back, Joshua went to the far corral and noticed Fireball was gone. Sheriff asked where his horse was. As he asked, John and Fireball were running back thru the field. Joshua said right there. John rode up fast and heavy. John made Fireball kick-up mud in the sheriff's face before stopping him. He dismounted and laughed, and said "Joshua, what did you think, I took off with him?" Sheriff Barnes said, "Who did you take off with, Mr. Black? John laughed, "With the horse, sir".

"I did not know you could be arrested for taking a horse for a ride!" John came down off Fireball and asked Joshua what was going on? Sheriff Burk said he had a few questions for him. You are John Black, correct. Yes sir, I am John Black. How can I help you? What time did you and Claudia leave the bar? Well, sir, I am not sure. We went to the parking lot, but Claudia did not want to enter the truck. She said she had just met me and would call me tomorrow, if that would be ok with me. I agreed and drove home alone. That was the last time I had seen her.

Why, what did she say I did, he asked. Sorry not much, she is dead replied Sheriff Barnes. What! John said. Claudia's body was discovered this morning just out of town heading towards the ranch. No! John replied. I left her in the parking lot last night. I needed to get home early to get up to train Fireball.

Ok John, did you see anyone around when you left her? No sir, I did not see anyone in the parking lot when I left her and drove off. Sheriff Barnes and Deputy Clark thanked him and told him to stay around for further questions they may have for him. John agreed, and said he was not planning to leave anytime soon. Sheriff Barnes and Deputy Clark left with Joshua. They all headed back up to the house. Heidi was waiting and crying with Butches wife on the front porch.

How could this happen here in their town they asked? Sheriff Barnes had no answer at this time. He tried to console and reassure them. Sheriff Barnes told them it was safe in their town. They all thanked him and Deputy Clark as they drove off. Joshua and Heidi were set back regarding this crime that was committed in their town. It was a peaceful town normally.

Maybe some locals would be drunk and hauled off to jail for the night on the weekends, that's all. What was going on? They just saw Claudia and had partied with her the night before. John was kicking himself, why did he hit so close to where he was staying. What was he thinking? He was not thinking, seeing those beautiful breasts. John was in prison for a long time and had no control over his urges. He had to react to them and he did.

John knew he did not have much time here after this and would have to speed things up sooner than he had planned.

CHAPTER 19

John needed to know when the Tripps were leaving. In addition, he needed to know when his workers were leaving as well. John Black needed the Tripps alone to himself so he could take care of them with no one looking for them. John saw Butch and Tom heading towards the barn. John stopped them and gave them a high five. "Hey guys getting a vacation. What are your plans? When do you ship off? I myself am jealous; I have nowhere to go. However, don't have any worries about me. I will be here when you come back. That means no extra work for you guys".

John asked Butch and Tom were they were planning on going. They said both of them and their wives' were going on a cruise to Jamaica. John asked when they shipped off. They were leaving tomorrow morning flying to Mexico first then boarding a boat there. Sounds like an awesome time John said. They all laughed and got to the day's work. Butch and Tom were singing island songs all morning. As Tom and Butch worked in the barn, John headed up to the house to question the Tripps on their plans.

As he reached the house, he heard arguing. Joshua and Heidi were discussing Claudia. As he approached the back door, he heard Heidi questioning Joshua's relationship with her. John knocked at the door before entering the house. He yelled "anyone home?" As he stood in the kitchen, he heard Joshua telling Heidi that he and Claudia were only friends. John yelled again "anyone home" and Joshua and Heidi both yelled "in here". They were in the living room. John entered the living room acting as if he just got there. John asked them if Joshua and Heidi were ready for their vacation. They looked at each other and said maybe.

John continued to ask where they were going for vacation. Heidi yelled maybe nowhere, and stormed out of the room. John and Joshua stood looking at each other waiting for one or the other one to speak! John went first and asked if this was a bad time? Joshua told him the Sheriff told him to stay in town right now. Heidi was thinking him and Claudia had a relationship going. John tried to console Joshua and said he would put a word in for him that he and Claudia were only friends. He went on to tell Joshua he had talked with Claudia at the bar and she never mentioned them having a relationship.

There was a knock at the front door. It was Sheriff Burk standing on the front porch. Joshua went to let him in. Sheriff Burk asked Joshua where he was last night again between the hours of 11:00 o'clock and midnight. Joshua told Sheriff Burk again he was at Nicky's place with Heidi and friends until 1am. Sheriff Burk informed Joshua he had questioned his friends and they remembered that he had been missing for a while that night. Joshua laughed and said he hit the bathroom for a while and then danced with Claudia in the back of the bar. He went on to tell him they did this because Heidi was very jealous of his relationship with Claudia and would have misunderstood them dancing. John interrupted and said he knew this was true. He went on to explain him and Claudia had many dances and conversation that night at Nicky's after her and Joshua had danced. Claudia was happy for Joshua and Heidi.

She had talked about how happy Joshua had been after meeting Heidi and marrying her! Joshua and Claudia's mother had been high school sweethearts. Joshua asked Sheriff Burk "Am I charged with anything?" Sheriff Burk said not at this time, but stay in town.

He asked if he could speak with Heidi. Joshua called her down stairs. Heidi entered the living room and said hi to Sheriff Burk. She asked if he had any new information on the case. Sheriff Burk asked her to sit down on the couch and asked Joshua and John to leave the room. They headed to the kitchen, grabbed some beers and took a seat at the kitchen table. Sheriff Burk went on to ask Heidi questions about their night at Nicky's Saloon. She told him they all arrived at 6 o'clock pm. They grabbed a table and placed their orders with Claudia. They ate and drank their share of booze and food. Then the band started and they all got up to dance, except John. He had no date that night.

Sheriff Burk asked Heidi what time they left the bar. She told him her, Joshua, Butch and Butch's wife stayed until closing. Tom and his wife left the bar around midnight. John asked Joshua to borrow his truck to head home around Midnight and Joshua gave him the keys to the truck. Are you sure about the times? Heidi said yes, last call was at 1 o'clock and it was just her, Joshua and Butch and his wife. They were the only couples left at the bar.

Sheriff Burk asked Heidi if Joshua and Claudia were involved. Heidi's face blushed with anger. She went on to tell Sheriff Burk that Joshua and Claudia were old friends that was all. Sheriff Burk thanked her and was getting ready to leave when his phone rang. He answered it. It was Deputy Clark informing him of new evidence in Claudia's case. He asked Heidi to excuse him as he went out to the front porch to finish the call.

Deputy Clark told him the DNA for Joshua Tripp did not match the DNA found on the body. He asked Deputy Clark if they had another match. He told him not at this time. Sheriff Burk re-entered the house and told Heidi to call Joshua into the living room. Heidi was scared, but called Joshua from the kitchen into the living room. Sheriff Burk said, Joshua had been cleared from being a suspect in the case. It was ok for them to leave on vacation, if they wished.

John was thrilled at the news. He now could finish his plan to get out of town with the Tripps money as well. John could live on their money for many years if he watched his spending. Sheriff Burk left and Joshua and Heidi asked John to stay for dinner. He accepted their invitation for dinner and left to get back to work. He needed to exercise Fireball yet and then wash and feed him. He was thinking when to make his move as he saddled him and took Fireball for a good ride.

John rode Fireball hard and strong for a half-hour. He would make his move tonight after dinner. No one would be looking for them for quite awhile, as they were due to leave for vacation. John returned with Fireball and washed him down after the long and hard run. John put Fireball in his stall in the barn and heard Tom and Butch saying their goodbyes to the Tripps. He heard Joshua and Heidi thanking them and wishing them well on their cruise. Joshua said, we will see you in 1 month, as we are taking a trip to Europe. Joshua told them their pay would be waiting for them when they returned from their vacation. Joshua was not worried that when they were away the ranch and horses would be well taken care of; he had made sure of that.

Tom and Butch hugged them both and said would see them in a month. Tom and Butch had worked for the Tripps for 15 years now. They could run his farm with their eyes closed. John joined them in the barn and told them all to have a great trip. He told them everything would run smooth while they were gone. Joshua told John he would not have to go it alone. Joshua had two men coming tomorrow to help with the ranch.

John was shocked, "dude I could have handled it myself for a couple of weeks!" We knew that John but we wanted to give you some help. You have proven yourself with how you handle Fireball and your work as well. We just wanted to make things easier for you. John you will be in charge of what they do. You are now the manager of the ranch while we are away. John thanked them both and said he would be up to dinner soon.

John knew now he had to stay around a least another week. The new help would be coming tomorrow and Sheriff Burk would be back as well. He still would be able to keep his plan of killing the Tripps tonight. John was almost done with digging their graves in the back west field of the ranch.

This would be a good spot to bury them, as it was full of pricker bushes; no one ever goes there. He would need to go out and finish this before going up for dinner. He went back into the barn to saddle up Fireball for the trip when Tom and Butch approached him. He had thought they were gone already for their vacation.

Hey, John just wanted to say goodbye again and will see you in two weeks, don't work to hard they said with laugher. Butch noticed John was saddling Fireball up. Hey, dude, why are you taking Fireball out? John laughed and said he needed to take Fireball to check the north quarter fencing. Joshua was concerned as there may be an opening there. They offered to help, but John said no problem he could handle it and have a great trip. John watched as they got in their trucks and left the farm.

CHAPTER 20

John mounted Fireball and headed to the west pasture of the farm. He reached it in less than an hour; he had worked Fireball hard. He was definitely a good buy. Fireball was born to run. He had reached his spot in the bushes and dismounted Fireball. John then looked for the shovel he had buried in the leaves earlier that week. He found it and continued to dig the graves for Joshua and Heidi Tripp. When John was done, he left to head back to the barn with Fireball.

He had wished him and Heidi could have shared the ranch together. However, Heidi was not going to leave Joshua. He put Fireball back in his stall and went to cleanup for dinner. When John arrived at the house, he could smell catfish cooking. This reminded him of home in Texas. It smelt wonderful and he was hungry from digging their graves.

John knocked at the kitchen door and Heidi yelled to come in. John entered the kitchen and saw Heidi fast at work cooking dinner. He told Heidi it smelt delicious. Joshua came in the kitchen and asked him what he wanted to drink. John asked if they had white wine. Joshua said that he had a bottle open in the dining room. John followed him into the dining room. The table was set with china and crystal, a centerpiece of lavender and baby's breath covered the middle of the table with six lit candles. The table was beautiful. He had never sat for dinner in this fashion.

Joshua poured him a glass of wine and invited him to sit down while waiting for dinner. John was feeling a little uneasy knowing his plans later this evening. Joshua asked him how he liked working on the ranch. John said he really enjoyed it, he really did. He was glad he had the opportunity to work there. John was feeling uncomfortable now knowing what he was planning to do. He had too! It was his time now.

They had everything, money, love, friends and the ranch. He on the other hand had nothing to lose. John, an ex-con, had nowhere to go! His family left him a long time ago and did not want him back. Hell, his dad had killed his mom three years ago. His father was serving a life sentence.

John had collected on his mothers insurance policies and headed out to find life. John found more than he planned on! He took life from young girls and women. He had gone on a killing spree over three states for six years. John Black was finally caught when he was only fifteen years old and had committed three rapes and two murders. John Black was sentenced to prison for 15 years for his crimes.

Due to his age, John was convicted as a minor and sentenced as a minor as well. John was remembering this as he killed the Tripps. John took a knife from the table and stabbed Joshua first; Heidi was shocked when John stabbed her husband in the chest. She ran for the kitchen to call the Sheriff. John was right behind her and threw Heidi to the floor.

Joshua was bleeding in the dining room. John tied Heidi up and went back to Joshua to see if he was dead yet. He was making gurgling sounds as John went over to him. Joshua was still alive so John pushed the knife in more and watched him die. John then went in the kitchen, grabbed Heidi by the hair, and dragged her upstairs.

John raped her for hours and enjoyed her screams. When he was done with her, he cut her throat. John went in to the bathroom and took a shower. When John was done with his shower, he went into Joshua's closet and picked out a shirt and jeans to wear. John then packed a suitcase with many of Joshua's clothes. John found a pair of black cowboy boots that were expensive and put them on as well.

He then returned to the bedroom were Heidi lay on the bed and wrapped her up in the sheets and dragged her down stairs. John returned to the bedroom to clean up. He remade the bed, went down stairs to wrap Joshua up in a shower curtain, dragged them out back, and dumped them into the bed of the truck. John then went back into the house to clean up the dining room floor, wash up the dishes, and put them away. When John was sure all evidence of the crimes was gone, he locked and closed the back door.

John drove the truck down to the barn where he had the horse trailer waiting with Fireball inside. He hooked up the trailer and drove to the site where he had dug the Tripps' graves. John threw Joshua's' body in first and Heidi's' on top of his and covered them up with dirt. John returned to the truck and sat there for a while rechecking his tracks that night making sure he had done everything he needed to, as not to leave a trace. When John was satisfied that he had, he headed for the highway.

CHAPTER 21

He now was Joshua Tripp, a very rich man. John decided to head up north. He wanted a nice small quiet town to set up residence in. John was getting hungry so he pulled of the highway for breakfast at a diner advertised along the highway. John went inside and sat down at the counter as a cute waitress came over to take his order. The waitress asked him if he was from around here. John said no, just passing thru.

John ordered eggs, sausage, pancakes and coffee. When the waitress came back with his food, she said she did not catch his name. John said he had not given it! John had to remember he was Joshua Tripp from now on. Joshua finished his breakfast and hit the highway again. He drove for days and pulled into a small town know as Salem in Massachusetts.

Joshua liked the town right off. He parked his truck and walked around town. He saw a real estate store and went in to find a place to live. A very pretty woman came to greet him. Hi, I am Sahara she said. How can I help you? Hi, my name is Joshua Tripp and I'm new in town, looking for a place to rent.

Sahara asked him what he had in mind, an apartment or a house. Joshua said he would like to rent a house out of town. Sahara told him she had two to show him. Sahara told him she could show him the houses this afternoon around three o'clock. Joshua said that would be fine and asked Sahara if she knew of anyone looking to buy a horse.

She asked him what kind of horse he had for sale. Joshua told her about Fireball. She told him to check at Cook's Ranch a mile out of town. Joshua thanked her and told her he would be back at three o'clock.

Joshua headed to find Cooks Ranch. Joshua drove up a long drive lined with white fencing along both sides where horses were grazing. He reached the main house and a tall man came out. "How can I help you?" the man asked. Joshua introduced himself to Jack Cook and told him about Fireball. They both went to the trailer to see Fireball as Joshua told him he hated to sell him, but could not take care of him anymore.

Jack Cook took one look at Fireball and said what a beautiful animal he was. What are you looking to get for him he asked? Joshua told him could let him go for ten thousand. Jack Cook stood and scratched his head; well I think we can do business as he shook Joshua's hand to seal the deal.

John told him to drive his truck to the corral down near the barn. Joshua parked the truck got out and headed to the trailer to unload Fireball. He put him in the corral and said his good buys. Joshua would miss him. Jack Cook told Joshua to come into his office at the side of the barn where he would give him a check for Fireball. With check in hand, Joshua drove back into town to find a bank to deposit all his money he was carrying, including the Tripps' money as well.

He parked his truck in front of Collins Real Estate

Store where he had to meet with Sahara at three o'clock. Joshua got out, walked down the street to Bank North and went inside to open a savings account. He went over to the information desk and told the women what he wanted to do. She told him to have a seat and Sue Todd would be with him shortly. Joshua took a seat and waited. Sue came over, introduced herself, and told him to follow her to her office. Joshua sat down in her office and told her he needed to open a savings account. Ok, Sue said, how much money do you need to deposit Mr. Tripp?

Joshua told her he had a hundred thousand dollars to deposit. Oh my! Sue said, that will not be a problem Mr.Tripp. Sue gave Joshua all the paper work to fill out and came back with a book and his deposit in it. Sue told him it was a pleasure doing business with him and said if he needed anything to give her a call. They shook hands and Joshua left the bank smiling, he was rich.

Joshua headed downtown to the docks where he heard about a great restaurant to have lunch. He found the Victorian Restaurant on the waterfront and went in for lunch. He was seated and looked over the menu sipping on a glass of red wine. Joshua ordered the day's special, baked Red Snapper and seaweed salad. His lunch was prepared well and tasted great. Joshua left the Victorian and walked along the waterfront checking out his new town. He was pleased with his new home.

Joshua thought as he walked how he had a great new start on life and needed to change his old habits of killing. He would be an upstanding citizen now. Joshua laughed to himself and wondered if he could change. He was sure going to try. He was rich and loved the small quaint town he would be living in.

Joshua noticed a clock above a store. It was two forty-five; he needed to head up town to meet Sahara. Joshua arrived at Collins Real Estate and Sahara was waiting for him outside. Hi Joshua, did you find Cooks Ranch ok she asked. Yes, Joshua said. Jack Cook bought my horse, thank you. They walked to Sahara's car and headed out of town to look at the houses for rent.

The first house was very small and needed a lot of work so Joshua passed on that one. They drove out to the next house, a log cabin with a great view of a meadow. Joshua liked the house and signed the contract, and moved in that afternoon. The house came furnished, so not much to buy. Sahara told him if he had any problems to call her.

She asked him what he planned on doing for work. He told her would be looking to work on a farm and did she know of anyone needing help. Sahara thought of Betsey and told him as matter of fact she did. She gave him Betsey's phone number and directions to the farm. He said he would give her a call, shook Sahara's hand, and said thanks for all your help. Sahara said my pleasure and they drove back into town.

Joshua drove to a food market across town that he had noticed when he entered the town. He needed to get supplies and food for his new house. He then drove out to his new home put his food and paper goods away, and went out to sit on his front porch with a cold beer. He loved how peaceful it was here. Joshua fell asleep on the front porch in the chair.

He awoke to a woodpecker pecking on a tree near the front porch. This was going to be a great life here; he could just feel it.

CHAPTER 22

Joshua's mind turned back to the present situation. Betsey and Joshua had finished their breakfast. Joshua was all filled in on the new lawyer for James. As they were washing up the breakfast dishes, the phone rang. Betsey nearly dropped a glass and ran for the phone it was Attorney Thornton. Yes, this is Betsey, how are you Attorney Thornton she asked. He said well and filled her in on his visit with James. He told her it went well but would be a hard case to prove self-defense.

The man that James killed was a lot smaller build than James, and much weaker as well. Betsey asked him if he would take the case. He told her he would and that James said hi and missed her. Betsey began to cry as he told her he would keep in touch with updates on the case, and when she could visit James again. Betsey thanked him and hung the phone up. She was startled by Joshua standing behind her.

I take it the news was bad, he said. She said looked bad but Attorney Thornton would still take the case. Joshua knew Betsey needed a day away from the farm so he told her to go get dressed for an outdoor outing. She smiled and asked him where they were going? He told her it was a surprise. While Betsey was getting dressed, Joshua filled a picnic basket with salami, cheeses, a loaf of French bread, grapes, cold macaroni salad and a bottle of wine. Betsey was ready and they took off for Joshua's house he had rented when he arrived in town months ago now.

Betsey did not know he had a house. He knew she would love it out there. As they drove up the driveway to his house, she asked where they were. Joshua told her at his house. Betsey looked puzzled and was surprised at how big the house was, a log cabin at that! She asked him how long he had lived there. Joshua told her not long and that he had rented it for a year. Joshua opened the door and started a fire in the fireplace; it was very cold in there.

Betsey brought the basket filled with food to the kitchen and put the food in the refrigerator. She was impressed at the size of the rooms and loved the kitchen. Joshua joined her in the kitchen and told her that is how he met Sahara, she rented him this house. Betsey was surprised that her best friend never shared that with her. Joshua went on to tell her that Sahara was the first person he had met when he came into town. She was nice and very helpful; they had formed a friendship right off. Betsey laughed and said that is Sahara all right!

Joshua proceeded to open the bottle of wine and poured two glasses. He asked her if she would like to join him on the front porch. Betsey took her glass of wine and followed him out to the porch. Joshua had brought two cushions out for the rocking chairs. They sat and looked over the meadow, drinking their wine and talking about the party they had coming up tomorrow for hayrides. Betsey was thrilled on how well their business was doing. A booking for horseback riding lessons or hay rides a week.

Things were going well, only if James could be there

to share in it Betsey thought to herself. They finished their glasses of wine and went back into the house for lunch. They brought their food and bottle of wine into the living room and sat in front of the fire to have lunch. When they were full, Joshua cleared the food away to the kitchen. While he was gone Betsey started to strip off some of her clothes. The fire was roaring and it was getting very warm. Joshua came back to see her sitting in her underwear and tank top in front of the fire. Her hair shined in the flames and her silk top sparkled. God she was beautiful, Joshua thought as he joined her.

They began to kiss which led to passionate lovemaking. They had fallen asleep in each other's arms. They were awoken as the fire had gone out and it was getting cold in the house. Betsey grabbed her clothes and dressed; Joshua did the same. It was four thirty and time to pack up their stuff. Joshua was taking her into town for dinner at the Victorian Restaurant he had lunch at his first day in town. Betsey told him he really needed to stop spoiling her. He said never!

CHAPTER 23

They arrived at the Victorian. They were seated and they looked over the menu. The waiter brought over an expensive bottle of wine that Joshua had ordered on the way in to the restaurant. They each ordered a cup of clam chowder to start. As they were finishing their soup, the waiter came to take their order. They both had ordered the stuffed striped bass.

As they left the restaurant Betsey told him she had a wonderful day! Joshua kissed her and said he was glad and he had as well. It started to snow on their ride home. Hopefully it would not amount to much; they had a hayride scheduled for tomorrow at 11 o'clock. As they reached the driveway there was a car parked up in front of the house. Betsey got out first to see Sheriff Burk knocking at her front door. Sheriff Burk heard them drive in, turned, and greeted Betsey on the porch. Hi Betsey I am here with new evidence on the Carlson's murder. Can I come in to talk with you, Sheriff Burk asked.

Sure, please come in and have a seat. Sheriff Burk came in and sat in the living room, the whole time keeping his eyes on Joshua. Betsey asked Joshua if he would go get wood and start a fire to take the chill out of the house. As Joshua turned to go get the wood, Sheriff Burk asked him how things were going on the farm. Joshua stopped in his tracks and did not want to talk with Sheriff Burk, but answered "very well Sir". He then headed for the back door to go get the wood. Sheriff Burk began asking Betsey how well she knew Joshua and his history. Betsey blushed and said she knew he was a good worker and great with their guests. In addition, he was a kind and gentleperson, why she asked.

Just asking Sheriff Burk replied! You know how some of us feel about new comers to Salem. Why Sheriff Burk, you were a new comer not too long ago yourself, she replied.

Sheriff Burk smiled and said yes I was! Getting back to why I came out to see you, we pulled up some fingerprints from the Carlson's bedroom, which do not match anyone in the family or the house cleaners. Have you found who they belong to yet? Betsey asked. No, we are still running it thru the system, no matches yet. This is the best lead we have gotten so far.

Joshua came into the living room with his arms full of wood and started the fire. As Joshua was starting the fire, Sheriff Burk started questioning him on where he came from and why he had moved here. Joshua was feeling very uncomfortable talking with him but not showing it! He had learned how to lie well, after spending his younger years in prison. Joshua answered his questions; he was born and brought up in Tennessee, on the Tripp Estate.

He had known everything about Joshua Trip from Joshua's wife. Joshua had attended the University of Tennessee for business, graduated and worked the ranch with his father and grandfather. Joshua married Heidi and they lived on the Tripp Ranch.

His parents had passed away in a car accident and

a year later Heidi left him for one of their ranch hands. They moved to Mexico, so he had heard. Joshua lied about Heidi leaving him but thought Sheriff Burk would understand, as his wife had left him for someone else! Sheriff Burk did understand and felt bad for Joshua! Sheriff Burk told Joshua he knew what he was feeling; it had happened to him as well. Joshua thanked him and said that is why he had to move on to somewhere new, a new start. Sheriff Burk now knew why Joshua had the bank account he had and did understand why he was here in Salem.

Joshua counted on the Sheriff's weak spot, a scorned man! Sheriff Burk left and told Betsey if he heard anything new he would contact her. She thanked him and said goodbye. Sheriff Burk yelled to Joshua, glad I finally met you. Joshua replied "as well you too sir". As Sheriff Burk drove down the driveway, Joshua felt relief the questions were over for now!

The fire was going well and giving much heat. Betsey went into the kitchen to get a snack and brandy for her and Joshua. Betsey returned with celery stuffed with cream cheese and bacon bits and two glasses of brandy to find Joshua sitting in front of the fireplace. He looked so at peace as his face and hair glowed in the flames. The smile on his face was somewhat eerie but peaceful all the same.

CHAPTER 24

Joshua was a very handsome man and mysterious as well. This is what kept Betsey drawn to him. Betsey went and sat down next to him on the floor and handed him a glass of brandy. Joshua said, why Betsey, are you trying to get me drunk and have your way with me! Betsey laughed and said what if am! He replied I would not fight you! They made love in front of the fireplace and both drifted off to sleep there.

Joshua was the first to awake. The fire had gone out and it was getting chilly in house. He checked the time it was 2:00 am so he woke Betsey and they went up to bed. Morning came fast for Joshua and Betsey. They woke to the alarm at 7:30am. The Martin Family would be arriving at 11:00am for their hayride and lunch. Betsey showered first as Joshua headed to the barn to feed and water the horses. Betsey came down stairs and could smell fresh brewed coffee. Have to love Joshua, she thought, he takes good care of me. She poured herself a mug of coffee and sat at the kitchen table going over the lunch menu.

Joshua finished feeding and watering the horses and headed to the house for coffee and a shower. Joshua came in the back door to the smell of fresh baked banana walnut muffins. Betsey was taking them out of the oven and putting them on racks to cool. Joshua poured himself and Betsey another mug of coffee and grabbed a muffin, almost burning his fingers. Betsey laughed, cannot wait can you? Your muffins, never Joshua said!

They both laughed and sat over coffee and muffins for breakfast. Joshua headed up to the shower and then had to go brush the two horses Jake and Sam for the hayride. He also had to load the hay into the wagon for the hayride while Betsey would be preparing the food for lunch. Joshua came down stairs hugged and kissed Betsey before heading to the barn again.

Betsey started to make buffalo chicken wraps with water crescent greens, scallions and cucumbers with a mayonnaise dill spread. She also had a bowl of Caesar salad with fresh crumbled blue cheese and croutons for a side dish. Betsey would now make dressing for the salad, which would contain olive oil, fresh chopped dill, ground black pepper, sea salt and a hint of sugar. This dressing would have to chill for 2 hours. Joshua finished brushing Jake and Sam. He was ready to start polishing the bridles for the horses when he heard someone in the barn.

He yelled "anyone there"? Alexis appeared. Hi Joshua, she said, could I help you with anything. Joshua told her to grab a rag and she could help polishing the bridles. They both sat and polished the bridles as Sahara was surprising Betsey in the kitchen. Betsey was surprised to see Sahara in her kitchen on a weekday. Sahara told her with Alexis starting spring break from school; she took the day off to spend it with her. She went on to ask Betsey if she could use her help doing anything for today's guests.

Sahara said that Alexis had run to the barn, as Alexis loved spending time there with the horses. Joshua loved spending time with Alexis due to how smart she was.

Joshua and Alexis finished polishing the bridles and Joshua asked her if she would help him bring Jake and Sam outside and harness them up to the wagon. Alexis was thrilled and said yes I would! She went on to ask him if she could ride upfront with him for the hayride. When Joshua said, I would be honored to have you as my co-pilot, Alexis's eyes lit up. It touched his heart!

Alexis was thrilled spending time with the horses she loved so much. Alexis also had a crush on Joshua!

Meanwhile, Betsey and Sahara were in the kitchen making homemade ice cream with fresh blueberries for dessert. Then Betsey and Sahara would prepare custard sauce to pour over the top of the ice cream. Joshua and Alexis had the horses all hooked up to the wagon and were driving them up to the office where the guests would arrive for the hayride soon. They made sure that Jake and Sam were hitched to the posts and ran up to the house to get something to drink before the guests arrived.

Betsey had made hot chocolate to put in a large thermos for the hayride and had extra waiting for Joshua and Alexis. They skipped into the kitchen laughing and singing one of Alexi's favorite songs, Born Free! Sahara was happy to see Alexis having fun with Joshua. She knew Alexis missed having her father around. Alexis' fathers' only contact with his daughter was birthday and Christmas cards.

Sahara knew Alexis needed a male figure in her life and here he was, Joshua, who she adored! They all sat at the kitchen table drinking hot chocolate and eating muffins. Alexis was going on about helping Joshua in the barn and riding up front on the hayride. Sahara and Betsey were happy to see her so excited about something, it had been a while that she was this happy. As they all were laughing and talking about Alexis' first experience hooking up the horses to the wagon, they heard the bell ring. Their guests, the Martin Family, were there for their hayride.

Joshua looked at Alexis and said its time to get to work dear! He and Alexis grabbed the thermos of hot chocolate and headed out to take the Martins for a hayride. Betsey and Sahara stayed behind to get the table ready for lunch.

CHAPTER 25

Meanwhile Sheriff Burk had called in the local State Police to help with the Carlson's murders. Sheriff Burk's department was not close yet to solving the case. Very little incriminating evidence was left at the scene. The medical examiner had confirmed Mrs. Carlson had been brutally raped several times before her death. No evidence of semen or DNA was ever recovered from her body.

The blood spatter was hard to retrace, as the person who committed the murders cleaned up well. In addition, he must have worn gloves. No pubic hairs where found on her body. This made it very hard to find the person responsible. He had left no evidence behind. If the killer had taken a shower after the crimes, he left no trace of blood. None had been detected in the showers drain. He must have cleaned up with bleach. He must have poured it down the drains of the sink and shower.

This contaminated any trace of the blood that possibly could have been retrieved from the drains. It would be unusable for the forensic team. The murderer was smart regarding leaving behind any evidence; he must have had forensics training.

Joshua and Alexis were having a great time with the Martins on the hayride. They were singing songs through the woods as they headed to the pond. The Martin kids wanted to stop at the pond. The Martins were vacationing from NYC and had never seen such beautiful woods as these.

The Martin kids had bought fishing poles at a store in town and they had hoped to use them. Bill Martin and his sister Mary begged Joshua to stop so they could try fishing in the pond. Joshua pulled the wagon over at the edge of the pond and got out to feed and water the horses. Alexis and the Martin kids hit the pond. Mr. and Mrs. Martin sat in the back of the wagon drinking hot chocolate watching their children having fun trying to catch fish.

After many bites on their lines with no success, the Martin kids were bored and they were ready to head back to the house for lunch. As they arrived back at the office, the Martins and Alexis got off to head into the house for lunch. Joshua drove the wagon with Jake and Sam back to the barn. He unhitched Jake and Sam, brought them back to their stalls, and continued back to the house for lunch.

Betsey and Sahara had them all seated at the dining room table and was serving lunch as Joshua arrived. They all sat down to a great lunch and conversation. The Martins were thinking of buying a summer place here in Salem. Betsey told them there's no better place to spend their summers. She had grown up here and loved every season, but especially summer on the island. If they needed help, Sahara could help them find the perfect home. Sahara explained how she worked at a real estate office.

How perfect was that for them! The Martins were staying on another two days and would stop in Collins Real Estate to meet with Sahara about summer homes to buy. Sahara told the Martins that would be great, say 1:00 o'clock tomorrow. The Martins confirmed 1:00 would be fine and will see you then.

The Martins said good-bye to Betsey and Joshua, thanked them for a wonderful time, and hoped they would be Salem residents this summer. Sahara laughed and replied, "Trust me you will be as we have many beautiful homes for sale".

The Martins thanked Sahara again for her help and said see you tomorrow at 1:00 o'clock. Before the Martins drove off, Betsey and Sahara were going over the properties that would suit the Martins. Joshua and Alexis just laughed at them and headed to the barn to tend to the horses and pick up after the hayride.

Joshua and Alexis put all the bridles and harnesses away then fed and watered the horses for the night. As they worked, Alexis told Joshua this was the best day ever! Joshua laughed and thanked her for her help; he said I could not have done it without you! Alexis smiled and said I know you couldn't. Betsey and Sahara were cleaning up the kitchen from lunch as Sahara told Betsey this day had been the best for Alexis. She told Betsey how much Alexis adored Joshua and being around him made her smile. Betsey was glad for Alexis and pleased with Joshua for including her in today's events.

CHAPTER 26

Betsey asked Sahara and Alexis to stay for dinner; they could make a day of it. Sahara thought that would be great but would help Betsey with dinner or no deal! Betsey agreed. Alexis and Joshua came in the back door singing Born Free again, laughing and teasing each other about who could sing better. Betsey and Sahara laughed and said neither one of them could carry a tune!

Sahara told Alexis about their plans to stay for dinner, she screamed yes! They all laughed and sat down at the kitchen table for some hot chocolate and homemade cookies. Alexis asked Aunt Betsey if they all could go horseback riding before dinner.

Betsey looked at Joshua and Sahara for their feedback on the idea. Joshua spoke first, why not, sounds like a great idea, he replied. Betsey and Sahara agreed as well so Alexis and Joshua headed to the barn again to saddle up the horses. Betsey and Sahara would join them soon down at the barn. They needed to change their clothes for the ride.

Betsey had clothes that Sahara could wear for the weather. They headed up to Betsey's bedroom to change. As they dressed, Sahara began to weep. Betsey asked her what was wrong. She said nothing, she was happy that Alexis was smiling and laughing so much today. She said

Alexis had not been this happy in a long time. Betsey went over to Sahara and hugged her, we're glad we could help and you know I love her too.

They finished dressing and headed to the barn were Alexis and Joshua were waiting for them with the horses all saddled up and ready to go. Joshua and Alexis both told them "about time girls!" They all mounted their horses and headed out to the north trail. This trail would lead them out to Quakers' quarry. The quarry was shut down now for 10 years.

It was a great swimming hole and make out place for the local kids. Betsey and James use to ride out there to look for pieces of granite. Betsey has some beautiful pieces on her coffee table in the living room. As they rode, they all sang camp songs. They came up to the quarry after one hour. They rode through the most beautiful woods. They dismounted their horses and tied them up before walking to the quarry's edge.

Joshua was fascinated with the quarry. He had found documentation at the public library in town. A serial killer known as the Butcher from the early 60's used it to dump his victims in the quarry. Six bodies were discovered there in the late 60's. Joshua asked Betsey and Sahara if the story was true. They said as far as they knew the stories were true.

As they all explored the quarry Sheriff Burk was busy trying to solve the Carlson's murders. He was checking on Joshua Tripp from Tennessee. He was on hold with the Sheriff's office in Fatback Tennessee.

Hi, Sheriff Burk How can I help you? This is Sheriff Burk, who am I speaking with? I am Sheriff Burk from Fatback Tennessee. I was calling you regarding a Joshua

Tripp, he replied. Is Joshua all right Sheriff Burk asked? Yes Sheriff Burk, he is fine and staying here in Salem. Then what do you need to know Sheriff? Sheriff Burk was not sure but had a gut feeling something was wrong with Joshua Tripp, but he had no evidence to confirm it.

Sheriff Burk from Salem told Sheriff Burk from Fatback he was sorry to waste his time but that they had a case they were working on; Joshua Tripp had been a new comer to town at that time. He was just doing a background check on him. Sheriff Burk from Tennessee told the sheriff Joshua Tripp was a good old boy, came from an upstanding family and would not cause any problems.

Salem's Sheriff Burk thanked him and again was sorry he had bothered him. They both said good-bye, but could not resist questioning why they both had the same last name. They both laughed and said it was a good strong name. They both shared a laugh! They went on to ask their first names. Thomas Burk from Salem, Jerome Burk from Tennessee. They continued to converse on family history and must not be related. Sheriff Jerome told Sheriff Thomas if he needed any other help to feel free to give him a call and they hung up.

The ground was still thawing around the quarry so finding pieces of granite would be hard this time of year. Joshua still looked hard for a new piece to give to Betsey. Betsey, Alexis and Sahara were throwing rocks into the quarry. Joshua had to laugh at them acting as if children would do. He kept his eyes on them for a while, noticing how beautiful they where and how much he loved all three of them.

He continued to search for a piece of granite for

Betsey as they played. Joshua kicked at the ground trying to uncover a great piece of granite. Then he spotted something shining a few yards in front of him in the sunlight. He ran towards it and kicked up the snow and there it was, a beautiful purple and pink piece of stone. Joshua then reached down, picked it up, brushed off the snow, and was amazed at its beauty. It reminded him of Betsey, she was the most beautiful women he had laid his eyes on.

Joshua spotted the pieces on the coffee table and knew this would fit right in with the rest. He put the piece of granite in his saddlebag on his horse. He then turned towards the direction of the girls to see they were still throwing rocks into the quarry. Joshua went over and joined them with throwing rocks. He enjoyed it! It was going on 4:0'clock now, time to head home before dark. If they left now they could make it by dusk. All saddled up and headed for Main Stay Inn.

CHAPTER 27

Betsey had gotten some fresh quail from Todd at the Birmingham's Market. Todd loved to hunt and would always call Betsey after he went hunting. Betsey had washed the quail and stuffed it with herbs, cranberries and garlic this morning. She had rubbed it with lemon juice, garlic, rosemary, sage and olive oil and placed it in a bag to marinate all day.

Sahara could help wash and peel the red potatoes to roast for dinner. Alexis could help with the fresh salad. Betsey would whip up some dressing for the salad. Olive oil, juice from an orange, garlic, fresh chopped shallots. Creole seasoning, ground black pepper and sea salt. They all reached the barn and dismounted their horses. It was getting dark and cold now, time to get the horses bedded down for the night.

Joshua and Alexis said they would take care of the horses. Betsey and Sahara headed up to the house to start dinner. As Betsey and Sahara entered the house the phone was ringing, Betsey ran to pick up the phone. Betsey answered the phone and James was on the other end. Hi, babe he said. How are you? I have missed your visits. She fell to the floor while telling him she had missed him too. He told her he was out of solitary confinement and could have visitors again. When could she come see him?

Betsey told her husband tomorrow she would be there and had a lot to tell him regarding the farm. James was thrilled at her response! He did not know what to expect after all this time, after what he had done to get himself into this mess.

His wife Betsey loved him for sure and he was the luckiest man on earth to have Betsey for his wife. They had met as teens and have always been in love with each other. James had a hard time being away from Betsey, he loved her more than life. He knew she felt the same but he knew for her this separation was much harder. After all, she had the farm to run and work on her own. James would not sleep all night just waiting to see her! Sahara came to check on Betsey, as she was gone awhile now.

Sahara found Betsey sitting on the floor below the phone. What happened, Sahara asked? Betsey told her it was James that had called. I can go see him again! Sahara helped Betsey up from the floor and hugged her with excitement. Sahara knew how much James and Betsey loved each other. They were sweethearts back in high school for god's sake!

Sahara and Betsey went back into the kitchen to finish dinner. Betsey's legs felt weak after her phone call with James her beloved husband whom she loved very much! Sahara told her to sit down; she could finish the dinner. As Betsey took a seat at the kitchen table Joshua and Alexis came in the back door of the kitchen. Joshua could tell something was wrong with Betsey. He went over to her and asked what was wrong? She told him she had talked with James.

Fear and jealousy ran thru him all at the same time!

He would not lose her again to a husband who only gave her pain!

Sahara and Alexis finished preparing dinner. As they all sat down at the dining room table for dinner, Joshua brought out the piece of granite he had found at the quarry for Betsey. Betsey was so excited at the piece! It was beautiful and was so different from the others she had. She ran and put it on the coffee table in the living room and returned to hug and kiss Joshua for finding it.

Alexis felt anger right now towards her aunt Betsey. How could she love Joshua and her husband too! What was it Aunt Betsey, James or Joshua? Alexis had a hard time holding her opinions with her aunt. Besides all the drama, that night dinner was great.

They had finished eating and Betsey thanked Joshua again for the beautiful granite piece. She still was amazed at how he found it with the ground covered in snow. He told her something was sparkling in the snow so he kicked up the ground underneath it and there it was the most beautiful piece of rock he had ever seen. Betsey agreed!

Betsey went on to talk about how she was going to see James at the prison tomorrow. Joshua was very upset with Betsey going to see her husband. He was sure with James killing another man she would have been through with him! What would it take to keep them apart for good!

Joshua sat and listened to Sahara, Alexis and Betsey talk about her visit with James. It took all Joshua had to keep a smile and participate in the conversation. He did have to give his feedback on the visit. Joshua told Betsey he thought ill of her going to see James; after all, he murdered two people! This upset Betsey and she yelled James is no murderer! You do not even know him!

Sahara and Alexis knew it was time to leave so they said their good-byes. Sahara told Betsey to call her after her visit with James. As soon as they left the porch, Betsey started yelling at Joshua. She wanted to know how he could have said such horrible things about James! Betsey told him she could not even look at him right now and stormed up stairs to bed. Joshua wished he had kept his thoughts to himself. He had seen how hurt and upset she was and knew he could not make her feel better right now. Therefore, he went into the kitchen to clean up after dinner and let Betsey cool off.

Betsey undressed and got into bed sobbing the whole time. Betsey had known her husband as a teen and he was no murderer! Betsey finally cried herself to sleep. Joshua finished cleaning up, poured himself a glass of brandy, and sat in the living room contemplating what his next move should be. Everything so far had failed keeping Betsey and James apart.

As Sahara and Alexis drove home, they talked about how upset Betsey had gotten with Joshua. They had wished none of this had happened and Betsey and James were going to bed together tonight. Sahara wished her best friend was not going through all this bad stuff and life was back to normal. Nevertheless, she knew this could never happen soon. When Sahara and Alexis got into their house, the answering machine was blinking. Alexis went over to check the message. It was Sheriff Burk wanting to speak with Sahara. What could he want to talk with her about?

Sahara knew it was too late tonight to call him back so she would stop by the station in the morning on her way into work. Alexis said goodnight to her mother and went up to bed. Sahara went to the kitchen to pour herself a glass of bourbon. After the night she had over at Betsey's she needed it to sleep. She wondered what was to become of Betsey with her playing two sides of the fence. Betsey had her husband James, who she adored, and Joshua her lover!

Sahara went through the clients she needed to see tomorrow, finished her bourbon and headed up to bed as well. Back at Mainstay Inn Joshua finished his brandy and had no clue what to do next regarding James so he headed up to bed. When Joshua walked into the bedroom Betsey was sound asleep with Kleenex all around her face; she had been crying!

This tore at Joshua's heart; he needed to end her pain. James needed to be dealt with! But how? Now with all that was going on with the Carlson's murders and James' last quest murdering the inmate that he had set up to occur. Joshua undressed and got into bed next to Betsey. He kissed her forehead, rolled over and went to sleep.

However, sleep did not come easily for him tonight. Betsey awoke at 4:30am, and jumped out of bed. She headed to the shower singing all the way knowing she could see James her beloved husband today. As she was drying her hair, Joshua awoke and went into the bathroom. He walked up behind her and hugged her and kissed Betsey's neck. Betsey was startled by this and swung around and pointed the blow dryer in his face.

"Back off Joshua, I am still not talking to you." Joshua, taken back by her reaction, put his hands up and walked backwards away from her. Joshua said, "Please don't shoot" as he laughed. Betsey found no humor in this! Joshua tried to apologize to her but she just left the bathroom and went to get dressed.

Joshua took his shower and would try at breakfast to smooth things over with her. He knew she could not resist him after a shower with Old Spice soap. Betsey dressed in James' favorite outfit, a royal blue velvet camisole top with purple lace, tight ripped jeans, her high black boots, and black silk tuxedo jacket. She then went down stairs to cook.

When she was upset, cooking was the only thing that calmed her. She hit the kitchen like a mad woman! Flour and eggs were flying all over the counter as she made bread and biscuits. Betsey started frying up bacon and sausage as well. Coffee was brewing in the coffee maker. Joshua got out of the shower to the smells of food cooking downstairs. Joshua knew when he got down stairs Betsey would be feeling much better than her cold reaction earlier with him. He knew cooking calmed her and made her feel better.

Joshua took his time before going down stairs. He gave her time to have coffee and sample the bacon and sausage and another mug of coffee first. As Betsey cooked, she kept an eye on the clock waiting to leave to see James. Joshua went down to the kitchen, and saw how involved in her baking and cooking she was and went up behind her and hugged her.

She turned around as he said how wonderful it smelt upstairs with her cooking. Joshua continued to apologize to her about his bad behavior last night. He told Betsey he had been out of line and was very sorry.

He continued to add he never wanted to hurt her and he loved her! Betsey could not stay mad at him; his sad face and he smelt awesome as well. She hugged him and told Joshua to sit down for breakfast. Betsey brought him a cup of coffee and started making an omelet for them for breakfast.

Her bread and biscuits had raised and were in the oven already. Betsey had purchased a dough machine in town for her new business. This would allow her to always have fresh biscuits' and bread every day.

Her omelets contained fresh mushrooms, goat cheese, tomatoes, basil, and scallions. After everything was ready, she served breakfast. As they sat at the table eating breakfast, Betsey told Joshua how he had really hurt her last night. Joshua again told her how sorry he was on what he had said. He only wanted to protect her from wishing too much for things that could not be.

Her husband was in a lot of trouble now and would not be coming home. This enraged Betsey as she had hope Attorney Thornton would get her husband's sentence reduced to 2 years. Joshua yelled at her. "In addition, how do you think this is going to happen? Are you blind to the evidence against him?" Betsey slammed her mug down on the table and yelled, "Whose side are you on?" Joshua replied "yours dear, of course. Remember, I love you and I am the one here for you not him!"

Betsey went on to tell Joshua James did not have a mean bone in his whole body and never would hurt anybody. You never knew him, she went on, I did my whole life! James is not responsible of the horrible things that they are accusing him of doing. Furthermore, in the end it will be proven self-defense on both cases. Ok Betsey, keep fantasizing this will happen, just remember who tried to keep you from getting hurt all over again! They finished their breakfast in silence after that.

CHAPTER 28

Sahara, awoken with her alarm, got up, showered and went down to prepare breakfast for her and Alexis. She was worried about Betsey and her meeting with James. She wished she could go with her but had three clients to see today and now Sheriff Burk as well. As she whipped up yogurt parfaits and toasted rye bread along with two hard-boiled eggs. Sahara knew Alexis would be down soon as she had heard her shower running when she was making breakfast. Sahara put breakfast on the table as Alexis came into the kitchen and sat at the table.

Sahara poured pomegranate and blueberry juice in their glasses and sat down at the table as well. Alexis could notice her mom was distracted and asked her what was wrong. Sahara told her daughter she was thinking about Aunt Betsey and her first visit with Uncle James after so long in-between visit's. In addition, what had happened after the last visit? Alexis tried to cheer her mom up by telling her mother about the Martins, who seemed to be an easy sale on a summerhouse. This would be a big commission for her mom.

Sahara kissed her daughter and headed off to work. Alexis was going to a friend's house for the day for a birthday party. Meanwhile, Betsey had taken the biscuits and bread out of the oven and started marinating steaks for dinner. She also had time to make a salad as well.

She was now ready to leave to visit James. Joshua was at the barn feeding the horses and cleaning their stalls. Betsey was ready to leave for her 3-hour drive to see James. She felt uncomfortable leaving without saying goodbye to Joshua. Therefore, she went down to the barn to say goodbye and let him know she had dinner taken care of already. She had steaks marinating in the refrigerator, cold potato salad with scallions and pickles, and mixed salad with olive oil and herb dressing.

He did not want her to go! Joshua grabbed her and hugged her as if he would never see her again. Betsey startled by his hug told Joshua she would be back before he missed her. He told her that could never happen! He said anytime she was out of his sight he missed her. Betsey hugged Joshua and said she needed to leave for the prison. He kissed her and said see you later babe! Betsey laughed and said see you soon and have a good day.

It was now 9:00am, Betsey got into her car and headed to the prison to meet with her husband, which was a good three-hour drive.

Sahara pulled into the Sheriff's station and parked. Sahara still was unsure why Sheriff Burk wanted to talk with her. She entered the building and asked to speak with Sheriff Burk. Deputy Carl told her to have a seat and Sheriff Burk would be right with her. Sahara thought it seemed like hours before Deputy Carl called her.

She was worried about being late for work now and just wanted to get this over with so she could go to work. Sahara had a busy day at work today; she had three clients to see. All could mean a good commission for her. She would finally be able to afford a nice vacation for her and her daughter. Finally, Sheriff Burk called Sahara into his office. He was right up front on why he wanted to talk with her.

Sheriff Burk thanked her for making time to see him. Then he went on to ask Sahara about Joshua Tripp. How well did she know him? Sahara asked why he was so interested in Joshua. Sheriff Burk told her he had a gut feeling there was something not right with him. What do you mean Sheriff Burk? Betsey and he are doing well with the farm and Joshua is great with my daughter.

I am telling you something is not right with him; gut feeling Sahara! Have you noticed anything weird about him with interacting with Alexis, or Betsey's friends? Sherriff Burk asked. All I have witnessed is Joshua treating Betsey and my daughter with respect and love Sheriff Burk. Why are you so interested in Joshua? Has he done something wrong that we should know about? No, just have an uneasy feeling about him, that is all, Sheriff Burk replied.

Sheriff told her about his conversation with Sheriff Burk in Tennessee. Sahara let out a laugh, "same name as you and same profession and title what are the odds of that," she said. Sheriff Tom Burk said, "It is weird and no we are not related before you ask." It seems that Joshua Tripp is a rich man. Family was very rich. Sheriff Burk went on to tell her that Joshua was married to his high school sweetheart as well. Her name is Heidi Tripp. She took off with Joshua's farmhand.

Sahara was feeling bad right now for Betsey. Betsey or Joshua never mentioned he had a wife! Thinking about it, its kind of funny Betsey has a husband as well. She had so many questions for the Sheriff with so little time to get the answers she wanted, as she was due at work in a half hour.

CHAPTER 29

Betsey had arrived at the prison and was waiting to meet with James. She was anticipating seeing him as handsome as he was. The guards brought a man into the visiting room that she did not recognize. Where was her husband James, she thought. This man could not be her husband! The man was pale and frail with no expression on his face. The guard sat him at her table and said only a half hour visit allowed. In addition, no touching allowed.

Betsey looked into her husband's eyes; they were dark and cold now. The James she knew was not there. Betsey reached out her hand to him hoping it might bring life back into him by her holding it; forget about the guards. James pulled his hands back away from hers. She asked him why he would not touch her.

James pushed his chair away from the table and called for the guard to come get him. Betsey was upset at her husband's reaction to her. She had waited so long to see him and touch his hand. Why was he being this way she thought. The guard came and brought James back to his cell as Betsey sat crying and wondering why he had treated her this way.

Betsey sat there for an hour before leaving very confused as she had just spoke with him yesterday and he was happy about being able to see her. Betsey got in her car for the long drive home. You see, Joshua had made a call to the prison earlier that morning and said he was James's long lost brother and needed to speak with him regarding an uncle that had passed away.

When James got on the phone, Joshua told him how he had been screwing his wife and what a great piece of ass she was. Joshua went on to inform him how long he had been sleeping with his wife and in James' bed as well! James was ashamed with himself. What had he forced his wife Betsey to do as to save their farm? He was disappointed with himself and with her as well for their behavior.

When the guard brought him out and he saw Betsey, how could he not speak to her? He noticed she had worn his favorite outfit. How many times had she worn it for Joshua? James felt bad leaving her sitting there like that with tears in her eyes, but dam it, she had been screwing another man in his home and bed! Moreover, here he was fighting for his life literally.

What had he done to his Betsey? She had always been the love of his life. She always stood beside him thru good and bad. Why now would she betray him in this way? Betsey had to pull over on the side of the road heading home. She was crying so hard her vision was blurred. Betsey pulled out her cell phone and called Sahara for some comfort as to finish her ride home.

Betsey had gotten her voice mail and left a distressing message! She briefly went into what had occurred between her and James during her prison visit with him. Betsey never felt more alone than she did right now. James had treated her like a stranger.

Was she a stranger to her husband now? James had

always been her whole life as well. Betsey had been his, so she thought. Did he know about her relationship with Joshua? If James did this could explain his behavior. Betsey was no angel now after sharing her bed with Joshua. How did James find out? She had never meant to fall in love with Joshua but she was alone and losing her parents' farm.

Her husband was in jail for murdering a man for at least five years and she was losing the farm! She asked, God how could James have done this to them? If anyone was to blame, it was James! Betsey began to wonder if she really had known her husband. James had killed again even being in prison for God sakes! Betsey composed herself and continued her three-hour drive home.

Back in Salem Sahara was showing the Martins two houses on the bay for sale. Joshua was tending to the farm and thinking about Betsey as he worked. He knew this visit would crush her and he wanted to give her a great night. Therefore, Joshua had made reservations at India West for them and her friends for 6:30 pm that evening. Hell he could afford it, as he was rich now thanks to the Tripps!

Sahara was showing the Martins the last home on the north end of town that was at the edge of the cliffs overlooking the bay. What a view, and the gardens surrounding the front yard to the cliffs were breathtaking! The old logging road that Joshua had used to dump the garbage bags from the Carlson's house was across the street from there. This Estate was known to have been that of Glendora Vamps, the daughter of Charles Vamps. He had been a very rich merchant here on Salem's Island. Charles Vamps had been a sea merchant who traded with many countries back in his day. Charles traded in fine silks and herbs from the Far East mostly. Their Estate was left to their only daughter Glendora, who was thought to be a witch by the locals.

She ran an imports clothing store in the downtown district. Fairies Delight was the name of her boutique. Glendora had imported silk and velvet clothing from European countries, much to the liking of the locals. Glendora had passed away in 1983 at her Estate surround by friends and family. The family Estate had been on the market for a year now. The locals say she still visits the cliffs in front of her Estate. Glendora was said to be seen naked at the cliffs edge on a full moon, as the legend goes.

The Martins were impressed with the house and grounds so they placed an offer on the house. Sahara was thrilled with the sale; it would bring her a big commission. Sahara knew the deal would go forward as the Martins could afford the house. Sahara followed the Martins back to the real-estate store to sign the papers. After she was finished with the Martins, she checked her messages. Sahara was shocked at Betsey's message!

Sahara tried calling Betsey back. Betsey heard her phone ringing and answered it. "Betsey are you ok?" she asked. Betsey began to cry again telling her about the visit with James. Sahara asked her how far she was from home. Betsey told her 1 hour. Sahara knew about Joshua's surprise dinner for her but did not mention it to Betsey.

Sahara told her she would see her later and they would talk it out. Betsey thanked her for always being there for her and would see Sahara later. Sahara told her to drive careful and would see her this evening. Betsey thanked her again and hung up.

CHAPTER 30

Sahara called Joshua to let him know Betsey's state of mind. He acted as if he knew nothing regarding Betsey and James' visit. Joshua was thrilled to hear James had reacted as he planned. His only concern now was Betsey. Joshua hoped she would be safe driving the three-hour trip in her state of mind. Sahara finished the paper work with the Martins and walked down to Neil's place. Nell was cleaning up the kitchen when Sahara came in the back door of the cafe. Nell was surprised to see Sahara. They hugged and Sahara began to tell her about Betsey's visit with James. Neil was very concerned for her friend Betsey! When Sahara told her about what had occurred at their visit, Nell became really worried about Betsey.

They agreed to meet earlier at India West restaurant to go over how to approach Betsey regarding her visit with James. They knew this would be challenging due to how Betsey would close her friends out at this time. Joshua was feeling great now, knowing that James would be done with his wife Betsey! His plan was working better than he had ever thought possible.

Why had he not thought of this before he had to kill again! Betsey was driving down her road to home. Her next turn would be the driveway to Mainstay Inn. She did not know how to tell Joshua why she had returned so soon. Betsey drove up the driveway to see Joshua waiting for her on the porch with flowers and balloons.

Betsey had forgotten it was her Birthday today! She was 31 years old today. How could she have forgotten? Her husband had as well! Betsey got out of her car, walked up the steps of the porch, and was met by Joshua. "Happy Birthday my sweetheart!" Joshua said. Betsey took the flowers and balloons and gave Joshua a hug and kiss. She asked him how he knew. Joshua said your friends are very informative when it comes to you.

They entered the house and Betsey started to cry again. Joshua took her in his arms and asked her what was wrong? Had he done something to hurt her? Betsey hugged him and answered not you through her tears. James had hurt her, she replied.

Joshua asked what James had done to make her so upset. Betsey tried to tell him but was too distraught to talk. Joshua walked her over to the couch and sat her down. He then went to the kitchen to get her a glass of brandy to help calm her down. Betsey took a sip and stopped crying. She sat on the couch in Joshua's arms for a while before speaking again.

She thanked him again for the flowers and balloons and told him she was glad for his thoughtfulness. She had forgotten it was her birthday with everything going on with James and the Carlson's murders. Betsey took a couple more sips of the brandy and was feeling much better now. She wiped her eyes and blew her nose before kissing Joshua for his gifts.

Joshua told her they could talk tomorrow about her visit with James. Today was to be filled with joy. After all, your birthday only comes once a year, he said. Betsey was silent and finished her brandy as Joshua told her that Sahara had sold the Martins the Vamps Estate at the north end of the island.

Betsey yelled "holy shit what a commission for Sahara! Good for her, she could really use this sale". Joshua told her that Sahara and all her friends were meeting at Indian West for dinner to celebrate. They needed to be there for 6:30 if she was up to it. Betsey sat in silence for a while before answering that would be fine. Although what she really was thinking was, she would like to jump off a cliff right now!

She had always loved her birthday until now! Winter was over and spring was on its way. What a better time to be born; everything has a rebirth this time of year. Joshua could see how exhausted she was and ordered Betsey to go up stairs and take a nap; they had a long night ahead of them. She did not argue with him and went up stairs to lie down.

Betsey tired and drained after her visit with James, went up stairs to bed to rest. Joshua was busy in the kitchen making raspberry and peach tarts for a night snack this evening for when they returned home from India West Restaurant. He had heard from Nell that was her favorite dessert and she had given him the recipe to make them.

As Joshua baked, Betsey slept for hours. Joshua finished the tarts and went to the cellar to get a bottle of champagne to chill as well for their nightcap. Joshua needed to get into town earlier than 6:30, as he wanted to go back to the shop where he had purchased Betsey's pink quarts ring. Joshua was going to buy her the necklace and earrings to match for her birthday. He and Sahara already planned for him to drop Betsey off at Collins Real Estate to help Sahara with something to do with fliers for the farm for the spring events. That would give him time to go shopping and meet them at India West for dinner.

Joshua went upstairs to wake Betsey to get ready for dinner. As he entered the bedroom, she was already up and out of the shower. As Joshua watched her dry off he could not keep his eyes off her, "god she was so beautiful". Betsey was startled when she saw him watching her and asked him if she could help him! He laughed and said "If we did not have to get ready to go out, yes you could," he replied! Betsey finished dressing in a chocolate chiffon velvet trimmed camisole, a pair of jeans, black velvet tuxedo jacket with tails and black boots. She opened her jewelry box and chose her mother's pink quartz and crystal necklace and earrings. Betsey was satisfied with her outfit and headed down stairs to wait for Joshua.

Joshua was just getting out of the shower when she had finished dressing. Betsey went into the kitchen to pour a glass of wine and knew she smelt her favorite tarts. She looked everywhere for them but did not see them. Betsey thought she was having a break down after her visit with James, so maybe that is what it was. She poured herself a glass of wine and sat in the living room near the fire. She was going over in her mind the visit with James. What possibly could have happened between the time she had spoken with him and her visit? Had he found out about her relationship with Joshua?

Betsey had planned to tell him about that at her visit today and explain how sorry she was for her weakness. How can she, now he won't even talk to her. What did he expect leaving her all alone? He killed a man instead of coming straight home after being at sea to see her! She was hurt and lonely as well as losing the family farm.

As she sat near the fire in deep thought, Joshua came down the stairs and stopped in his tracks at Betsey's beauty. She was amazing to him, her beauty, and the outfit she was wearing hot! Joshua approached her. She was in deep thought as he kissed her on the check. Betsey, startled by this, jumped and laughed. She told him she was sorry but had been in deep thought about her life. Joshua smiled and said you look amazing my love! Betsey giggled and pushed him away and went to the kitchen to pour them both a glass of wine before leaving for dinner. Betsey returned with the glasses and sat down next to Joshua in front of the fire. Betsey told him how awesome he was looking as well.

He was suited up in a black tee shirt with a gray moon and black tree on it, black jeans and a silver belt buckle with a tree embellished on it along with a black blazer and cowboy boots made of alligator. It was funny how their style of clothes and conversations were on point. Betsey knew how this was playing with danger, but they seemed to fit like a glove together.

This became reality today with her visit with James, so called visit! Joshua told her it was time to leave for town now, as Sahara would be waiting for her. Therefore, they brought their glasses to the kitchen and headed into town. With their ride into town, they sang to the radio all the way. Rock stars they were not, but they enjoyed singing anyway. Joshua dropped Betsey off at Sahara's work place and headed downtown to the waterfront to purchase her birthday gift. Joshua knew he would make it back before dinner.

Betsey got out at Collins Real Estate. Joshua told her he would miss her but he was going to grab a coffee at Nell's while he waited for her and Sahara. He told her that they would meet at India West Restaurant. Betsey squeezed his hand then thanked him again for her birthday plans and got out of the truck to meet with Sahara.

CHAPTER 31

Sahara was waiting for her at the door and grabbed Betsey in a bear hug. Betsey said, "hey no one died you know!" Sahara pushed back Betsey's beautiful red hair and whispered in her ear "Happy Birthday to You!" Betsey hugged her as well and laughed. Alexis came from the back of the office singing happy birthday to Aunt Betsey as well. She was carrying flowers and a gift in her arms. Betsey took the flowers and gift from her niece Alexis and gave her a hug and kiss. They both told her how beautiful she looked as Betsey began to cry again!

Sahara and Alexis both hugged her and said everything was going to be fine with time. Alexis grabbed a box of Kleenex and handed it to her aunt. Betsey dried her eyes and blew her nose saying she had to freshen up her makeup before they left for the restaurant. Sahara walked Betsey to the bathroom in the back to freshen up.

Betsey was telling Sahara that she had not received a card or phone call from her friends this year. Sahara told her not to worry, they still remembered her birthday and she was going to see them all later. Betsey hugged Sahara and Alexis, and told them how much they meant to her and thanked them for the flowers and gift. Alexis told her aunt Betsey she had not opened the gift yet. Betsey laughed and said you are right I have not done that yet.

Betsey opened her gift that was beautifully wrapped and saw a beautiful crystal and blue topaz necklace in sterling. Betsey hugged them both and said how much she loved the necklace. Betsey put the necklace in her purse, as they were ready to walk down town to the Restaurant.

As they walked, Sahara told Betsey anytime she wanted to talk about her visit with James she was there for her. As well as all her friends, as they felt the same way. Betsey thanked her and said, not right now, she needed to forget it for a while. Sahara took her hand and said we all love you and support you in anything you do. You do know that I hope, Sahara asked. Betsey told her she knew her friends were there for her and was grateful for that. However, she was not ready to talk about it yet.

They continued walking downtown to India West in silence. As they entered the India West, Sitar the headwaiter brought them to a private room in the back. There were balloons and flowers everywhere. At the front of the room was a table with a cake shaped like the Mainstay Inn along with horses running in a pasture. It said Happy Birthday Betsey. Betsey began to cry again for the fifth time today. All her friends came for a group hug. As they broke their hugs, Betsey spotted Joshua coming into the room. She went to him and greeted him with a long lasting kiss that made his toes curl up.

Wow, he replied, you did not miss me did you? Betsey laughed and said always! If it was not for you, the farm would have been sold and I would be all alone, except for my friends of course. She laughed, as they could not do the things you have done for me! Joshua actually blushed for the first time in his life.

He really loved her, heart and soul. Betsey brought

out the best in him in every way and he never wanted this feeling to end. He would do anything not to lose his Betsey. Joshua had already proven this with the murdering of the Carlson's earlier this month and Joshua's conversation with James this morning. It would seal the deal.

They all sat down at the table set for their party of seven and drank wine with many different types of finger foods before dinner. Betsey and Joshua were holding hands under the table and Betsey could not ask for a better birthday than she was having today. All her best friends and niece as well as her newest friend Joshua surrounded her. He has been so great for her and her family's farm.

He has always been there for her in these bad times with strength, support, and love. She is realizing her husband James will be gone at least five years or even more for his crimes. This scared her very much. Children would not be in their future at that point in their lives. As they all drank and ate, the night was magic for Betsey. Dinner was done and everyone began to give his or her gifts to Betsey. Betsey sat and opened all her gifts with Joshua at her side helping with the paper.

She had received many great gifts. As she came to the last card, it said to my soul mate with love. Betsey was hoping it was from James. She opened it and saw the necklace and earrings that matched her ring that Joshua had given her earlier that month. Betsey looked at him and gave him a kiss and hug for his gifts. Betsey's heart was hurt; her husband had not sent even a card for her birthday.

Betsey thanked everyone for being there on her birthday as well as her gifts. They all continued drinking and reminiscing about their childhood with much laughter by all. Joshua was amused at what the girls had done as children in Salem. He laughed right along with them as if he had been there.

Joshua never had a childhood so he enjoyed living through theirs. It was 9 o'clock and the party was winding down. Betsey and Joshua said their goodbyes to everyone, as the party was over; it was late. Joshua told Betsey he would be right back; he needed to go settle the bill with the restaurant manager for the party. Betsey grabbed his arm; she never expected he was paying for this on his own. All her friends were here as well. Joshua told her not to worry he had invited them and could afford it. Anything for his sweetheart, he continued to mention, as she deserved it.

Betsey was overwhelmed by the day's events. She thanked him again for the best birthday ever. Joshua laughed and said the night was not over yet! He had also set up an appointment with a tattoo parlor for her and him to get a tattoo tonight. As they left the restaurant, they walked one block down to Misty's tattoo shop. Joshua took Betsey's hand and led her into the shop. Betsey, who was scared, asked why we are here Joshua? He told her he had scheduled her to get a tattoo for her birthday.

Betsey was shocked and surprised at the same time. How did Joshua know she had wanted to get another tattoo? Betsey was getting a fairy tattoo on her lower back, and Joshua Betsey's name on his forearm. It was 11:30 pm when they had finished getting their tattoos.

As they walked to Joshua's truck, they stopped in a bar called Gillian's. It is where Joshua had parked his truck. When they entered the bar, a band was playing Irish Rock music. They took a seat near the windows overlooking the square, where there were many shops of different merchants.

Joshua ordered a bottle of Merlot wine and an order of fried calamari as well. They sat, drank, and ate again. In addition, they talked about the many guests they had out to the farm since their first guest.

Things were going well for Betsey and Joshua now. They had finished their bottle of wine and calamari and headed for home.

CHAPTER 32

Betsey and Joshua arrived at Mainstay Inn around 1am. They entered the house to find a fire roaring in the fireplace and the house warm. Joshua was glad Sahara and Alexis had no problem starting the fire for him. Betsey was wondering how the fire was going as they had been gone for the evening. Joshua had to fill her in on how he asked Sahara and Alexis to stop on their way home to start the fire for them. Betsey was overwhelmed by the kindness of her friends and Joshua today.

It had started out to be the most horrible day ever and then turned into the most wonderful day ever! Joshua told Betsey to sit by the fire and he would be right back. He went in the kitchen to find Sahara had baked the tarts and left them cooling on a rack. He placed them on a plate, put a candle in one tart, and lit the candle. Joshua then grabbed two glasses and the bottle of champagne and headed back into the living room where Betsey was waiting.

Betsey was in deep thought again, still trying to figure out why James did not want to talk to her today. Betsey smelt the raspberry and peach tarts under her nose. She was surprised that Joshua had gone through the trouble of getting the recipe and making them for her. They sat and enjoyed the tarts and champagne. The fire was roaring in the fireplace. It could not have been a better birthday for Betsey. She told Joshua how pleased she was with her birthday surprises.

They had finished the tarts and continued to drink their champagne with conversation regarding the spring events at Mainstay Inn. Spring was only a few weeks away now. The Martins would be moving into their summer home soon and this would bring many of their family and friends to the area. Things were looking up for Betsey except she could not share it with James; this broke her heart! Joshua could see Betsey was still upset after her visit with her husband and wanted to make her pain go away. How could he compete with the ghost of James! Joshua thought he had up until now.

After Betsey's last visit with her husband, she was going into a deep depression now. He would need to start all over again erasing her feelings for James. Joshua was up for the challenge, as he loved her with all his heart. After all, he had killed for her more than once. Joshua knew that soon Betsey would be seeing things his way. Joshua was the only one to offer her a great life now, filled with love, passion and money.

As they finished their champagne, sleep was in order for both; as they were tired from their long day's events. They headed up to bed for sleep only. All though Joshua expected more but thought ill of it due to Betsey's mood.

The alarm went off at 5 o'clock the next morning. Joshua was up, took a shower, and headed for the barn to care for the horses. Betsey lay in bed thinking about James and not wanting to get out of bed. Why was her husband treating her in this way? She had used mostly all of her parents saving to get him a good lawyer and tried to keep him out of jail. James was the one who gave away their life, as they knew it! He was the one, the one who violated their love for one another! Betsey admitted to herself that sleeping with the first man to come along was wrong and hurtful, but she had been confused and lonely for some time now after James' conviction.

Betsey needed that connection with a man again. Joshua was different, full of compassion and so much passion and love for her she could not help herself for taking it. After all, she was left with the fall out of trying to save the farm. She had already lost too much with losing James; she could not bear losing the farm as well. Betsey lay in bed crying about her decisions she had made up until now, knowing there was no going back from the things she had done.

Another year older and still so far away from her lifetime plans. Betsey and James had spoken about having children to fill their lives and raise them on the farm. Betsey as a child and teen had many beautiful memories growing up on farm. She had the horses to take care of and she rode them in many local competitions as well. This farm was her life!

Betsey knew by the time James would be released from prison, her dreams of having children would be very slim. This depressed her even more now. Betsey knew she had to get up and make breakfast for Joshua and her lying here would not change the future or bring her old life back! Betsey dragged herself out of bed and headed to the bathroom to take a shower and dress for the day.

As Betsey was showering, she was thinking about being another year older and soon her body would not look the same. This depressed her even more. She finished bathing and dressing in tight jeans and a royal blue velvet camisole with an open black sweater with studs. Betsey put on makeup and headed down to the kitchen to start breakfast. As she entered the kitchen, fresh coffee was ready for her in the coffee pot. Joshua really took good care of her! Betsey poured herself a cup of coffee and began to cook breakfast for the two of them.

She made eggs, asparagus, tomatoes, goat cheese and lamb omelets. As Betsey was finishing cooking the omelets Joshua came through the back door from the barn. He grabbed her kissed her and said you look beautiful my love. Joshua asked what smelled so good. Betsey told him she was cooking omelets for breakfast.

Joshua sat down at the table for breakfast, he had noticed Betsey's unusual mood. He could see she looked preoccupied so he tried to bring her mood up by telling her a joke. What happened to the goat who spoke he asked. Betsey said she had no idea. Me either Joshua said! They both laughed and finished their breakfast. Joshua was glad he was able to make Betsey laugh at least once today.

In the meanwhile, Sheriff Burk was calling the Carlson's murders a cold case. The Sheriff's department had come to a brick wall on the case. All the evidence they had collected was of no use in solving the case. Whoever was responsible for the murders was not on the database system for criminal history or wanted list by the FBI. Sheriff Burk was frustrated by this set back and would have to let Betsey know about the case going dry. He knew this would be no help for her husband's cases against him. They had thought this would help his case regarding someone setting him up for the murders.

Sheriff Burk was heading to Mainstay Inn to give her the news as his radio came in with news of a garbage bag with suspicious contents in it that the Martin boys had found at the north end of the island.

The Martins arrived three months in advance to their new summer home. The Martin boys were exploring their new house and property when they saw a green garbage bag bobbing up and down in the surf at the edge of the cliffs in front of a cave. They worked their way down the cliffs to the opening of the cave. There they had found the garbage bag bobbing in the surf. The boys pulled it in to the shore near the cave above the cove. The Martin boys opened the bag, saw the bloody clothes, and called the Sheriff's office.

Sheriff Burk arrived at the scene within a half hour. He took the bag and saw the bloody clothes. Sheriff Burk called in his forensic team to the scene. They combed every inch from the cliffs edge to the base of the cliff as to collect further evidence. The day was good for retrieving evidence, as it was calm and sunny, no rain or wind.

The Martins were uneasy about buying a house in Salem now. Mr. Martin called Sahara regarding the situation going on near their house. Sahara told him this never happens here in Salem and was so sorry for the situation regarding their new home. Sheriff Burk tried to reassure them about what was happening around their new home as well. He informed them this was an isolated case and never was a regular happening here in Salem. His town was normally quiet and peaceful.

The town of Salem always was a perfect town to start

new roots in. It had always been a beautiful spot to live and raise children. This was a quaint town where all had lived in peace up to now! Betsey and Joshua were out in the barn grooming the horses, not knowing of what was unfolding in town. Sahara tried to call Betsey to let her know about what was happening in town. She got Betsey's answering machine and left a message for Betsey to call her immediately!

Betsey and Joshua were having fun in the barn. They found an open stall and jumped in kissing and groping each other as they lay down in the stall. This then led to clothes being torn off along with passionate, wild sex!

Betsey and Joshua rolled in the hay for what had seemed like an hour before coming up for air. Then, they were startled by a voice yelling if anyone was there. Betsey jumped up and immediately got dressed as Joshua was trying to do the same but was still excited by their time together that had been unfinished. He was finding it difficult to get dressed at this point. Betsey could see this and laughed, "Sorry babe I cannot help you at this point, take a rain check?" she asked! Joshua could only laugh at that. He loved her even more at this point.

As Joshua was getting dressed, Betsey was out in the barn already to see who was there. Betsey ran into Nell out in the main barn. Nell had stopped to see how Betsey was doing after her visit with James yesterday and how her birthday was as well. Nell could tell her friend Betsey was very upset at dinner and had worried about her all night. Nell had known Betsey's dreams about having children and raising them on her parent's farm, as she had been. Nell could only be there for her now with whatever she needed.

Betsey and Nell hugged as Joshua came from the back of the barn. Nell blushed and said she was sorry for intruding on them. Betsey blushed as well and said she was glad to see her. Betsey and Nell went up to the house while Joshua finished up in the barn before heading up to the house to join them. They had time alone for Nell to question Betsey about the things going on in town and with James before Joshua came up to the house to join them. Nell could see Betsey was glowing after her time with Joshua, she knew they must have had sex for sure! Any women would know that look! That look is always unmistaken by another woman. Betsey blushed as they sat at the kitchen table to talk. Betsey could not hide her feelings for Joshua.

Betsey went on to tell Nell about her visit with James yesterday at the prison. Nell let her know that all her friends knew what had happened to her at that visit. Betsey wanted to know how they could have known, before she had told them. Nell said she had heard about Betsey's phone call with Sahara on her ride home from the prison. Betsey accepted that and continued to tell her about her visit with James. What Betsey did not know was Joshua had called her husband prior to her visit to see him and disclosed all what they had been up to in the bedroom!

As Betsey and Nell talked, the phone rang and Betsey ran to answer it. It was Sheriff Burk. He let Betsey know the case with the Carlson's had been considered a cold case up until today. He explained where he was and what the Martin boys had found. Sheriff Burk continued to inform her that the contents in the garbage bag were definitely from the Carlson's house. This could be the break in the case his department was looking for. Betsey could only hope this would lead to more evidence to help James, as to prove his innocence and that it was self-defenses in both cases against him. As Betsey talked with Sheriff Burk Joshua came in the back door to find Nell sitting at the table alone. Joshua asked where Betsey was. Nell said the phone had rung and Betsey went to get it and was still on the phone.

Joshua's body went limp thinking it could be James and him telling her about a conversation with him regarding their sex life together. As Joshua entered the living room, which adjoined the hallway where the phone was, Joshua heard Betsey saying thank you Sheriff Burk please keep us informed with any new evidence. Joshua startled Betsey when he ran into the foyer where Betsey was on the phone. Joshua asked Betsey what was wrong. Betsey told Joshua it had been Sheriff Burk and that he had come across new evidence for the Carlson's murders. Joshua was feeling very uncomfortable at the news. He was hoping he had left no DNA behind. Joshua was not ready to move on and leave Betsey; he loved her more than life itself! Joshua could see himself with her for life, children and all!

Joshua was done running from the law; he had met his soul mate who was worthy enough to be his wife. He was hoping on a family with Betsey and all of them living on the farm.

Sheriff Burk was convincing the Martins they had chosen a great place to buy. He went on to tell them of all the events year round on the island that drew many from afar. Salem was a great place to relax and enjoy all it had to offer. The Martins were feeling better about their choice of places for a summer home now and thanked Sheriff Burk for coming so quickly to their son's call. As Sheriff Burk was leaving the Martins, Sahara arrived to help with smoothing over the events of the day.

Sheriff Burk said hi to Sahara as they passed in the driveway of the Martins Estate. Sheriff Burk had been fond of Sahara now for a year, but afraid to ask her out on a date. Sahara felt the same towards him. Sahara was thinking of Betsey and her courage and ran back to ask Sheriff Burk out for dinner tonight. Her asking him out, he had wanted to do the same, but a woman asking him shocked Sheriff Burk! He swallowed his pride and said yes, would love to. They agreed to meet at the Victorian House at 6:30 pm.

Sahara was nervous, so she called Betsey for help. Betsey answered the phone to Sahara yelling in the other end, "I have a date"! You and Joshua have to come to town for dinner tonight at the Victorian House, please say yes! Why, what is up with you, Betsey asked. I had the nerve to ask Sheriff Burk out to dinner Sahara replied. Betsey was so proud of her and said they would be there for her at Victorian Restaurant this evening. Sahara thanked her friend and said that she would see her later.

Sahara had to go shopping to buy a new dress for dinner. As Betsey hung up the phone, Joshua came around the corner and asked what was going on. Betsey told him about her conversation with Sahara about her date for tonight. Joshua was uneasy having dinner with the Sheriff but agreed for Betsey's sake. He knew how much her friend meant to her. They both went up to the shower to get ready to go out for dinner.

Joshua knew this would give him an opportunity to

get Betsey in the shower with him. They both got in the shower to save time, which took longer than they both had intended! Joshua scrubbed Betsey and she scrubbed him. Betsey had ridden him like a horse she had to break; Joshua ran his hands through her hair and fondled her breasts. Betsey and Joshua made love, grinding, caressing, and with much pleasure. They had enjoyed each other for an hour before finishing their shower.

They dressed, having a hard time keeping their hands off each other, and went down stairs to leave for dinner. Betsey remembered she had forgotten to take her birth control pill. Betsey did not remember if she had yesterday as well. Betsey and Joshua left for town for dinner with Sahara and Sheriff Burk at the Victorian. Betsey was excited for her friend Sahara having a real date. She had always hoped Sahara would find someone so Alexis could have a father.

Betsey's expectations were high for her friend tonight. Sheriff Burk was young, handsome, had a good job, and would be able to support a family. Betsey would make sure everything went well for the date. Joshua and Betsey arrived at the Victorian House before Sahara and Sheriff Burk so they went in, took a table at the window, and waited for Sahara and Sheriff Burk to arrive.

Joshua ordered two bottles of their finest champagne to help with the evening ahead of them. As the waiter brought the champagne to the table, Sahara and Sheriff Burk arrived. Everyone introduced him or herself again to each other and enjoyed a glass of champagne. Joshua had ordered eggplant, oysters and clam appetizers to start the night off. They talked, and were enjoying each other's company as the waiter came to take their order.

Joshua and Betsey already knew what they were having. They were going to split a rack of lamb. Sahara and Burk decided that sounded wonderful and ordered the same. The waiter took their order and asked if he could get them anything else? They all said they were fine and thanked him for asking. Betsey noticed Sheriff Burk and Sahara were getting along well already, as she had thought they would! The conversation was light and cheerful while waiting for their main course.

Betsey and Sahara were telling them about them growing up in Salem with many humorous stories, which kept all laughing. Joshua was shocked at how wild Betsey had been as a teen. To Joshua, Betsey seemed grounded and very responsible. He had imagined her as a very studious student, glasses and all. Sheriff Thomas Burk found Sahara charming and smart; her looks were great as well. He really admired her for working two jobs and raising a teen on her own.

The waiter came with their dinners that looked as good as they smelt. They all enjoyed their meal and finished with nightcaps of brandy. They all were having such a good time they left the Victorian House Restaurant and stopped at a local coffee shop and purchased coffees, and then Joshua and Thomas went into the Spirit Store for a pint of brandy to add to their coffees.

They walked along the waterfront talking about upcoming events in town that they would like to attend. They all agreed to attend some of them together. A horse and carriage had pulled up to the curb were it dropped people off so they hopped on for a ride around town.

It was a beautiful night, clear skies and warmer temperatures. As they approached the Main Square, with many shops and restaurants that lined the cobble stone street, they got off to go through the shops. As they walked, they ran into the Martins. Sahara had sold them the old Vamps Estate. They all said hi as Mr. Martin pulled Sheriff Burk aside and asked how the investigation was going with the bag of clothes his sons had found at the water's edge down from their new home. He told Mr. Martin that it was an ongoing case and could not discuss it at this time. Jeff Martin understood this, but was hoping for some special favor as he was an attorney in NYC.

Sherriff Thomas Burk tried to reassure him that he and his family were in no danger. Joshua was unsettled at them talking alone among themselves. He needed to keep on top of any information regarding the bag that was found by the Martin boys. After all, he dropped it over the cliff! Thomas and Jeff returned to the group shortly after leaving to talk. They all agreed to hang out together, going through the shops, and then end up at Gillian's Pub for drinks. As they walked through the shops, the girls stuck together as well did the men. Betsey, Sahara and Beth Martin tried on clothes and jewelry. The men talked about their favorite sport teams.

As they finished the last store, the men were carrying all the bags of goods that the women had purchased. They arrived at Gillian's Pub around 8:30pm. They were all seated at a table at the front window were they could look out over the Square. The waiter came to take their order as Joshua spoke up and said he would pay for their drinks. Jeff and Thomas thought he was showing off for the girls, but accepted his offer. They all agreed on a couple of bottles of Merlot for their choice. The waiter left to the wine cellar to get the wine.

He returned with two bottles of their best and six wine glasses. The waiter opened the bottles, and poured a little in a glass for Joshua to try it to see if it was to his liking. Joshua had no clue if this was a good bottle of wine or not, but had to act as if he did. Joshua Tripp was a wealthy ranch owner and should know about fine wines. Joshua was very nervous now; he took a sip and said this will be fine, thank you. Joshua only hoped everyone else would agree! Especially Jeff and Beth Martin, who were very rich and could have blown his cover as being the rich horse rancher from Tennessee.

All were pleased with the selection and the conversation went to Joshua and his life before Salem. Joshua felt like he was sitting in the hot seat and began to perspire as being in the spotlight. Joshua went on to tell them the last year was very painful for him, as his wife had left him for another man before they were to travel around the world. They all felt bad asking him to talk about such a bad time! Joshua was glad the discussion had moved on from him.

Joshua hated to talk badly about Heidi Tripp, as she had been a sweet girl. Sweet was putting it mildly. She was beautiful and had a great body and soul. He hated that he had to kill her too. He knew she loved her husband Joshua and could never be happy with him. Especially after he killed her Joshua! He did what he had to as to survive in this world. Now he was rich but would someday be on the run again from the law, this he knew.

CHAPTER 33

In the meanwhile, back in Tennessee, the farm hands had returned to the Tripp ranch to start work after their cruise. They were very confused to find it vacant and Fireball was gone. Where were the Tripps, John and Fireball? A month had come and gone now; they should be back by now from their trip.

Tom and Butch were worried about Joshua and Heidi and Fireball being gone. They spoke with the hired ranchers, who were taking care of the ranch for the Tripp's during their time off. The men told Tom and Butch that the day they had arrived, Fireball was not there. They had just assumed the Tripp's had taken him along on their trip or sold him. They explained the horse trailer was missing as well.

Tom and Butch were very concerned now! They headed up to the house to check to see if the Tripp's had returned home and left again for the day. As Tom and Butch reached the main house, they noticed no cars in the driveway or around back. They could see Joshua's truck and trailer were missing as well. Tom and Butch knew they did not take the truck or trailer to the airport. They checked the house, no doors or windows were tampered with. Everything was intact. They really began to get worried, as John Black was not there either! He was to stay on to work the ranch. What was going on!

Tom decided to call Sheriff Burk to see if his office had any news on the Tripp's. Sheriff Burk answered and asked Tom what was wrong? Tom went on to tell him what him and Butch had found on returning to the ranch after a month's vacation. Sheriff Burk told them to calm down that the Tripp's were fine. He explained to them that he had spoken with a Sheriff in Salem Massachusetts who knew Joshua. Joshua had ended up there to avoid coming home due to Heidi taking off with another man.

Tom and Butch were very shocked at this. They had know Heidi and Joshua for years and said, "no not Heidi"! This was not right, something was definitely wrong! Joshua and Heidi adored each other. Joshua had been gone for long periods buying horses and Heidi had never strayed. They knew this as they and their families would keep her company as so she would not be lonely when Joshua was away. Sheriff Burk told them that Joshua was in Salem, Mass and Joshua did not know or care where Heidi was at this point!

Tom and Butch were not convinced with the news regarding their boss. It did not add up. They could feel something was not right with this situation. Joshua would have called them if not Heidi. They went down to the barn and took care of the horses, but were stilled worried about the Tripp's. Sheriff Burk had not convinced them that Joshua and Heidi were no longer together anymore. Meanwhile Joshua {John Black} was having a goodtime with Betsey's friends. They finished the bottles of wine and all headed for home. They all agreed to meet for the town's first event. They would make a day of it. They all said their goodbyes, hugged, and headed for their cars.

The Martins had the least distance to drive, just down the road. Sahara and Thomas left first to head out of town to Sahara's place, which was a few miles down the road from the Mainstay Inn. Betsey and Joshua left right behind them. Joshua followed Sahara and Thomas all the way home. They tooted their horns as Joshua pulled into the driveway of Mainstay Inn.

Betsey was wondering if Sheriff Thomas would be staying at Sahara's for the night. They seemed to hit it off quite well. Joshua told Betsey to mind her own business concerning Thomas and Sahara. If Sahara wanted her input, Sahara would have asked. Betsey laughed and asked when he became so smart on romance! He stated I do well in the matters of the heart! Betsey had nothing to reply to this. Joshua was a great lover, cook, and very romantic all in one. Joshua was right; she had nothing to say about their relationship, Sahara was an adult. They entered the house; it was chilly so Joshua went to start a fire in the fireplace. Betsey headed upstairs to change. She was wondering what was happening at Sahara's house right now. Betsey hoped great sex, as she had experienced with Joshua. If not, any sex would do, as Sahara has had none for years, after her husband left her for a younger girl from Chicago.

Back at Sahara's house, she invited Thomas in for a cup of coffee and he accepted. As they were drinking their coffee, Alexis awoke and came down stairs. She was pleased to see her mom with a nice man, any man at this point! They both said hi to Alexis and asked if they had woken her up? Alexis wanted to sit with them, but laughed and went back upstairs to bed. Grown-ups, yuck! Sahara and Thomas talked and found out they had many of the same values that they wanted in their lives. Thomas and Sahara began to kiss on the couch, which lead to going upstairs to Sahara's bedroom.

It had been a long time for both of them as Sahara's husband had been gone a year now and Thomas had lost his wife to another man a year ago also. Sahara and Thomas seemed to remember what to do! They rolled in bed for hours not wanting to stop; it had been so long for both to enjoy sex. They seemed to feed off each other and enjoyed the moment.

Sahara awoke to a knock on the bedroom door and it was light out; must be morning. It was Alexis checking in on her mother, as she never slept in this long. Sahara jumped out of bed, grabbed her robe, and went to the door opening it slightly. Alexis was standing at the door and Sahara told her she would meet her in the kitchen. Sahara saw Thomas still asleep in her bed and she remembered their night together. She smiled and went into the bathroom and started the shower. As she took her shower, the shower curtain opened, and Thomas got in with her. Sahara felt uncomfortable at first, but enjoyed his company quickly!

Both showered, dressed, and went down stairs to face Alexis in the kitchen. Sahara was not looking forward to the confrontation with her daughter on her behavior last night. Thomas was feeling nervous as well. They both felt like high school kids again! Alexis was waiting at the kitchen table drinking a cup of coffee. "Well", she said, "it was good of you two to get up". Sahara and Thomas both were blushing at her comment. Alexis was glad for her mom and really liked Sheriff Burk.

Alexis got up and poured them both a cup of coffee and told them to sit down; she would make them breakfast. Sahara was shocked at her daughter's reaction to her and Thomas spending the night together. Sahara gave Alexis a wink and said that would be wonderful. As Alexis made breakfast, Sahara and Thomas talked over their coffee on what they could do today, as they did not want their date to end yet. It was Saturday and both did not have to work today. They decided to call Betsey and see if she and Joshua wanted to go horseback riding out to the quarry. They asked Alexis if she would like to join them, but she declined as she had plans with friends. They all sat and ate Alexis's wonderful breakfast over great conversation and many laughs.

Sahara went to the phone to call Betsey as Thomas and Alexis cleaned up after breakfast. Betsey answered the phone to Sahara saying good morning on the other end. "I hope I did not interrupt anything", Sahara said. Betsey laughed and said "no we have been up for hours now". Betsey said she could not wait to talk to her as she had called an hour ago and Alexis said that you were still sleeping in with your guest! Sahara blushed again and told Betsey she had been right and Thomas was wonderful. Betsey told her "I gathered that due to him sleeping over on the first date" as she laughed! Sahara told her to hush and asked if she and Joshua wanted to go horseback riding out to the quarry today with them?

Betsey replied how did you know we were planning to do that today, Sahara? I did not know, Sahara replied. Betsey went on to tell her the Martins had called earlier this morning asking the same question, as they were expecting friends to arrive today on the ferry from NYC, and would like to go horseback riding as well. Betsey could not see any reason that Sahara and Thomas could not join them as well so they agreed to meet at Mainstay Inn at 12:00 sharp.

Betsey told her she expected a full report on her night with Thomas. Sahara giggled and said maybe; see you later, as they hung up. Betsey could not wait to tell Joshua she had been right about wanting to fix up Sahara with Thomas. Joshua was down at the barn getting the bridles and saddles ready for their guests today. Betsy, who could not wait to tell Joshua, headed to the barn to gloat. Joshua had told her not to get involved in matters of the heart with friends. Was he ever wrong this time! As Betsey approached Joshua in the tack room of the barn, he could tell she was very pleased with herself before she spoke.

What brings my beautiful lady down here, should I ask! Betsey just smiled and told him he would have to eat crow as her date matching was right on. She quickly told him how Thomas and Sahara had spent the night together and would be joining them today for horseback riding. Joshua was surprised that the two of them had committed on the first date. This new relationship could either help his deceiving and his new identity or help them find out his real identity. Joshua hated to be in this situation; dam Betsey and her nosey friends! Really, of all people, the local Sheriff! Why could Sahara not have found a good old farm boy for her mate? Why did it have to be the Sheriff in town!

He was upset with Betsey but acted pleased with her wanting to fix up Sahara with Thomas. His love for

Betsey was clouding his judgments now. Joshua needed to bond with Sheriff Burk and Jeff Martin, as they could help shield him from all his crimes. What better friends for an ex-con and murderer to have! Joshua and Betsey finished up with the saddles and bridles for today's ride and headed back up to the house for coffee and donuts. When they entered the kitchen, the phone was ringing. Betsey ran to answer it. Joshua was thinking now what! Betsey answered the phone to Sahara's voice, hi Betsey, calling to ask if we could bring dessert today to have after the ride. She explained to Betsey they were driving into town so as Thomas could go home and change clothes. They were going to stop at Nell's to get dessert. Betsey told her that would be great, as she had nothing ready for the last minute booking from the Martins. Beth Martin did tell her they were heading out to Mainstay Inn after lunch.

Sahara and Thomas went into town to his house so he could change clothes. Sahara was surprised at how nice his house was, nice furniture and decorated great as well. After he was done changing they drove downtown to Nell's for lunch and to get dessert for Betsey's house later. Nell was surprised to see Sahara and Sheriff Burk holding hands at a table in her restaurant. Nell told Jess her waiter she would take their table. Nell went over with menus to Sahara and Sheriff Burk's table. Welcome Sahara and Sheriff Burk Nell said, as she handed them menus while smiling at Sahara with a wink. What brings both of you here today, Nell asked? We are on our way out to Betsey's place to go horseback riding and needed some lunch. I also need to bring dessert to Betsey's for after our ride. No better place than Nell's for lunch and purchasing dessert, Sahara replied. Nell smiled and said good answer my friend.

Sahara and Thomas ordered Nell's special of the day, corned Beef with Swiss cheese, lettuce, tomatoes in a wrap with Thousand Island dressing and pan-fried lightly with cucumber salad. After they had finished their lunch, Sahara asked Nell what she had special for dessert to bring to Betsey's, as she needed enough for eight people. Nell said she had just made a chocolate and black cherry truffle with Mary Oliver frosting. Sahara and Thomas agreed that would be a great choice, so Nell went to box it up for them. As Sahara and Thomas were leaving, Nell pulled Sahara aside and asked her what was going on with Sheriff Burk. Sahara blushed and Nell knew. "Oh my god Sahara, you go girl'! Nell hugged Sahara and then said goodbye to them and said she would call Sahara soon. Thomas and Sahara started their drive to Mainstay Inn for horseback riding. They should arrive on time 12:00 sharp.

Back at the Mainstay Inn, Betsey and Joshua had just finished lunch and were ready for their guests. Betsey finished filling wine pouches for the ride. Betsey had three goatskin pouches to carry wine in for their trip; they would fit in the saddlebags and would be enjoyable when they reached the quarry. She also packed cheeses, crackers and grapes for a snack to go with the wine. As Joshua and Betsey were walking down to the office, Sahara and Thomas pulled up. Sahara got out first with the trifle that she needed to bring up to the house. Betsey said she would go with her.

Thomas got out of the truck and was glad for the alone time with Joshua, as he still found something uneasy about him every time he was around him. Joshua, not liking this situation being alone with the town Sheriff, was afraid he might slip up with something in conversation. Betsey was interrogating Sahara about her night with Thomas. Sahara was blushing telling Betsey about their lovemaking, the best sex she had in years! Sahara told Betsey how Thomas felt the same and wanted to be a couple. Betsey yelled yes! As they were going over every detail, Joshua rang the bell at the office; the Martins and their friends had arrived. Joshua could not be more relived at seeing their SUV pulling up in the driveway. Betsey told Sahara they needed to finish this conversation later. They both laughed and headed to the office to meet the Martins and their friends.

They all mounted their horses with Joshua and Betsey helping them, then started down the trail to the quarry. All were enjoying their ride through the scenic woods to the quarry. They all had spotted deer and a timber wolf along the way. The Martins' friends from the city were really enjoying the woods and animals they were coming across. They finally reached the quarry an hour out.

The Martins and their friends were amazed at how beautiful it was here, and they were glad to stand on solid ground! They all explored the quarry and sat down on a blanket Betsey had brought for wine and snacks. They sat and drank wine with cheeses, crackers and grapes. Conversation was on the history of the quarry and surrounding woods mostly. Jeff Martin had read years ago about the serial killer who had used this quarry as his dumping grounds for his victims. All the girls were getting spooked so they changed the subject quickly. Joshua was upset. He was enjoying hearing about the stories of the victims that been buried here. It helped him relive his murders and this aroused him! Joshua felt empowered by this.

Thomas was watching Joshua during the tales of the quarry and it confirmed his concerns about him. There was something not right about this person! Thomas's gut was telling him to watch Joshua Tripp closely, very closely! They finished the snacks Betsey had packed for the ride and the stories as well. It was time to head back to the farm, as the Martins had dinner plans with their company later in town.

On the ride back to the inn Jeff Martin tried to stay up front with Joshua as he needed more one on one contact with him to disclose his personality fully. The girls all talked the whole ride home. Clothes and fashion was the subject. Beth Martin was telling Betsey she needed a makeover. Beth would love to take her to NY City for one. Betsey declined and told Beth she was happy with who she was and how she dressed. Betsey thanked her anyway. Sahara chimed in; she would love to go to NY City for a makeover! Betsey and Beth both laughed. Beth said to Sahara, she would be glad to take her. Betsey asked Beth if she knew what she was in for taking Sahara to NY City! Beth laughed and said no, not at all!

Jeff Martin was trying to interrogate Joshua with no success. Joshua was quiet about his life and Jeff Martin could not break through that determined silence. Joshua either had a horrible childhood or was hiding a secret. Martin's gut feelings were right regarding Joshua, he just knew it! Jeff Martin and Thomas Burk both felt uneasy around Joshua. They were waiting for him to explode and not in a good way but an evil way. Joshua had all the personality and traits of a troubled man.

They arrived back at the barn at 5:30pm just before dusk. Martin and Thomas helped Joshua to unharness the horses and put them in the barn for the night. The girls went up to the house to warm up. Joshua began to feed and water the horses so Jeff and Thomas helped Joshua to bed down the horses as well for the night. Joshua thanked them for their help. The men had finished taking care of the horses and headed for the house as well.

Joshua knew Jeff and Thomas were not comfortable around him. He planned to take everyone into town for dinner as to flash his wealth as Joshua Tripp would have done. Maybe if he acted the part of a self-raised rich boy, they would back off! As they entered the kitchen, the girls were sitting at the kitchen table laughing about how horrible some other women looked. Joshua said he would like to take their new friends and old ones out to dinner in town tonight. They all looked at each other in surprise, accepted his offer, and thanked Joshua for his invitation. He went on to say why end a perfect day with great friends; we will bring it into this the evening as well.

Betsey said she would make a pot of coffee and have some of Sahara's dessert she had brought. In addition, so they could warm up before heading into town. All said that would be great. Joshua said he had a few more things to do at the barn and would be up soon. Everyone else sat and drank coffee and ate dessert and talked about what a great day it had been. The air had been cool but the sun was warm; spring was on its way.

Betsey excused herself to go up stairs and change for dinner. Betsey asked Beth and her girl friends as well as Sahara if they wanted to freshen up. They all said that would be great and followed Betsey up stairs. Thomas,

Jeff, and the other men sat at the table and discussed how they felt something was wrong with Joshua. Their gut feelings were saying something was not right. However you cannot go on just gut feeling! Thomas and Jeff were aware of this, as both men were in professions that pertained to the law.

Sheriff Burk was still waiting for pending evidence found at the Carlson's home. Jeff Martin's sons fished it out of the cove earlier this week. All this evidence may help catch the killer. Joshua was well aware of what Jeff Martin's sons had found. He only hoped the rough surf had gotten rid of his DNA, if any had been left on his clothes, along with James' file. The waves below the cliffs were rough churning waters washing away anything in their path.

The women were coming down stairs as Joshua came in the front door with more wood for the fire. Joshua told the girls he did not think they could look any better! They all laughed and Betsey hit Joshua in the arm almost causing him to drop the wood. Jeff and Thomas heard the laughter and went into the living room to join the girls and Joshua. Joshua placed some wood in the fireplace to light later on their return from town. All headed for their cars to go into town for dinner. They would all meet at the Victorian House.

Everyone arrived at the same time and went inside for dinner. Joshua asked the waiter to bring three bottles of their best champagne. "Yes, sir right away"; the waiter was impressed with his order. The waiter returned promptly and poured glasses of champagne for all. John asked if they were ready to order. Joshua said they would start with some appetizers first. They would have an order of clams casino, fried eggplant and fried calamari. All were pleased with his choices. The waiter left to put in their order and asked if he could get them anything else. They all said they were fine for now. As they enjoyed their appetizers, talk was about the Martins' new summerhouse and their plans with the remodeling of the estate. Joshua told Jeff he was very handy with carpentry and would love to help Jeff out. Joshua was trying to get friendly with the enemy. Jeff thanked him and said he may take him up on his offer.

Beth and Sahara were planning a trip to NY City and Betsey decided to go as well. It would be fun watching Sahara in a big city! They were to leave in two days. The men were feeling left out. They asked if the invitation was open to them as well. Jeff said he had something to finish up at his office in the city before he started their vacation in Salem. Joshua and Thomas were on board with the idea of seeing the city as well. How could the girls say no to their men! Therefore, it was set; all were going to NY City.

Betsey and Joshua would have to find someone to take care of the horses while they were away. Betsey would ask Mr. Green who lived down the road from her. Mr. Green always told her if she had needed him, he would be there for her and James. The waiter brought their dinners and they ate and talked about what they would do in the city. Joshua thought this would be a good time to bond with Jeff and Thomas. As they all left the restaurant, Jeff said he would book rooms at the Hilton in Manhattan as he was friends with the manager and would get a good rate for their stay. Sahara said she would call the airlines and book their seats and everyone could pay up the day they leave.

Everyone said good night, thanked Joshua for dinner, and left for home; it was eleven o'clock already.

Meanwhile, back in Tennessee, Tom and Butch were running the Tripp ranch and still not buying Heidi and Joshua breaking up. They needed to speak with Joshua so they went into town to the Sheriff's office to find out how to get a hold of Joshua. Sheriff Burk in Tennessee was gone on a fishing trip and would not be back for two weeks. Tom and Butch would have to wait, not liking it at all. They both felt something was very wrong!

CHAPTER 34

Betsey and Joshua got home at midnight and were ready for sleep. It had been a long day. Joshua started the fire as Betsey went to the kitchen to get them a nightcap, two glasses of brandy before bed. It would take the chill off and help them sleep after their exciting news, their trip to the big apple. They talked about what a great day it had been with the Martins, Thomas and Sahara. Betsey was excited now about going to NY City, as Joshua would be coming with her.

Thomas dropped off Sahara at her home. They both were very tired and not up for a repeat of last night so they made plans to meet in town for coffee before work tomorrow. Sahara went inside to find Alexis sleeping on the couch and woke her up to go to bed. Alexis told her mother she was very happy for her and Thomas and hugged her mother and went up to bed. Sahara followed her daughter up stairs to bed as well. Sahara would tell Alexis tomorrow about her New York trip. Sahara would have to call Alexi's friend Julie's mom and ask if Alexis could stay with them while she was away.

The Martins had brought their nanny with them from New York City, so their boys, would be taken care of while they were gone.

Joshua was awake, he showered, and then grabbed a

cup of coffee and went down to the barn to feed and water the horses, as Betsey was still asleep. Betsey awoke to the smell of fresh brewed coffee and went down to the kitchen and noticed Joshua was gone to the barn already. She looked at the clock; it was eight o'clock already, she had slept in. Betsey went back up stairs and showered, dressed, and went back down stairs to start breakfast. She was making crêpes with spinach, goat cheese and tomatoes. Toasted rosemary bread with apple butter as well. Joshua came in the kitchen door raving about the wonderful smells coming from the kitchen. He poured another cup of coffee and sat down for breakfast. As they ate their breakfast, conversation was about their trip to New York and things they wanted to see when they arrived there.

Sahara arrived at the Candy Café; she was meeting Thomas there for coffee. Thomas had arrived before Sahara and ordered two coffees and bagels with eggs and bacon on them for both of them. Sahara was surprised; this breakfast had been her favorite for years. She and Thomas had much in common. As Sahara and Thomas sat eating their bagels and drinking coffee, their conversation was about the trip to New York City and how excited they were to be going together.

Meanwhile Jeff Martin was contacting his office regarding his arrival back in New York and having his secretary book rooms at the Hilton for his friends. Beth was also on the phone to her decorator to come back with her to redo the Vamps Estate for her.

Betsey and Joshua had finished cleaning up after breakfast and Betsey was going up stairs to start packing for their trip before going over to see Mr. Green to ask him if he could tend to the horses while they were away.

Joshua went down to the barn to let the horses out in the pasture for the day.

Sahara and Thomas hugged and kissed each other good-bye and both headed to work and would meet later at Sahara's for dinner. The Martins were excited about showing the city to their new friends. Jeff and Beth were planning on places to bring them. Betsey arrived at Mr. Greens at ten o'clock; he was pleased to see her and invited her in for ice tea he had made this morning with fresh mint. Mr. Green was pleased to help Betsey with the horses and glad she was getting away after what was happening in her life right now. Betsey thanked him and left for home. Betsey wished she could see James before she left but she had spoken with James's lawyer and James did not want her to visit. The lawyer told Betsey he was working on getting a new trial for James. Betsey could only hope this would happen and James would get out of prison. Betsey arrived home and went down to the barn to let Joshua know Mr. Green would take care of the horses while they were away.

She found him in the tack room polishing the harnesses for the horses and sat down to help him. They finished up with the harnesses and went up to the house for lunch. Betsey had made a crabmeat salad while cooking breakfast. She would serve it over salad with old-fashion coleslaw dressing. Homemade ice tea spiked with hard cider as well. Betsey served lunch and Joshua could not be more amazed at her talent for cooking. After lunch they went for short horseback ride and went back home to finish packing for their trip.

Sahara got out of work early and went to Birmingham's Market to get steaks for supper for her, Thomas and Alexis.

She also picked up three potatoes for baking along with a bag of salad. Sahara headed home to prepare dinner.

Sahara was excited about having a man to make dinner for again! Sahara got home at 4: o'clock and put down her bags from the store on the kitchen counter seeing she had a message on her answering machine. She played the message; it was Thomas saying he would be late for dinner. There was new positive news regarding the Carlson's case that needed his attention. He told her he should only be one hour late would be his guess, sorry, and could not wait to see her and Alexis later. Sahara, a bit disappointed, put the steaks in the refrigerator to marinate and put the salad in a bowel, topping it with some fresh herbs, and put that in the refrigerator as well. As Sahara saw it, more time for the food to marinate the better it will taste!

She went up stairs to check on Alexis to see if she was doing her homework. Sahara found Alexis hard at work on her homework; she was very proud of her daughter. Alexis said "hi mom, home early?" Yes, I have some good news for you. Thomas is coming over for supper. Oh great, what are we having?. Sahara told her daughter, "What! I'm good at cooking!" Alexis laughed and said steak and baked potatoes! Nice guess she told Alexis.

Alexis asked her mother what she needed to tell her. Sahara did not know how to start the conversation about going to New York City with Thomas and her friends. Sahara just blurred it out! Me, Thomas, Betsey, Joshua and the Martins will be going to New York City for a couple of days. Beth Martin is going to take me for a makeover! Alexis squealed with amusement thinking of her mom in New York and a makeover! Stop, Sahara told her daughter, that was Aunt Betsey's reaction as well!

When are you leaving? Sahara told her the day after tomorrow. Alexis could not believe her mother was leaving so soon. Sahara tried to explain to her daughter that it happened so quickly she had no time to say no. Everyone was set on going now!

Meanwhile back at the Sheriff's department, Sheriff Burk was reviewing the evidence from the lab regarding the bag found at the old Vamps Estate. There was not much to go on because the rough current around the rocks had washed away any DNA that could have helped the case. They did recover washed up paper though. The lab was trying to analyze it and piece together what it contained. The paper was soaked and the print was unreadable, so they were going to send it off to the FBI for their help. Sheriff Thomas had allowed the delivery of the evidence to the FBI office in Boston.

Thomas knew this would be a closed case due to the little evidence they had collected so far regarding the Carlson's case. One more day till New York City; he could use to get away. He had been putting in many hours since the Carlson's murders.

Meanwhile back in Tennessee Butch and Tom were wondering where John Black was. They knew something was wrong and needed to find out what it was! Moreover, why did John Black leave the ranch? Something was very wrong; they just knew it! All Butch and Tom could do at this point is wait for Sheriff Burk to return from his fishing trip, as to contact Joshua.

Back in Salem, Betsey and Joshua were leaving for town to shop for their trip and have lunch at Nell's. Betsey wanted to pick up some new sweaters and pants for the trip, Joshua as well needed pants and shirts. They also would shop for new jackets as they were told it would be chilly in New York City.

They both wanted fashionable jackets for the city. Betsey went into the Blue Moon Boutique were she found most of her clothes. Inside she found the coat she was looking for, a long black cream-colored leather coat fully lined with sheepskin. She was also able to purchase two pairs of pants and three sweaters. Joshua was amazed on how fast she found what she had been looking for! Betsey paid for her purchases and said your turn Joshua. He had no clue where to shop for what he needed, as he was not familiar with the men's stores in town. Betsey said she knew exactly where to take him. Vamps store for men's designer clothes. It was located down at the waterfront.

The Vamps, who had owned the Vamps Estate, also had owned Vamps clothing store. After the last Vamp had passed away, it was sold and the new owner kept the famous name for his business, as it had been well know worldwide. Joshua had no problem finding clothes there as well as a coat that matched his girl Betsey! The burgundy trim matched Betsy's hair. They had finished shopping and went to Nell's for some lunch. As they were waiting to be seated, Sheriff Burk and his deputy arrived for coffee. They talked awhile about their trip as the waiter called the Tripp party for lunch.

Deputy Carl asked the Sheriff if this was the person he was interested in for the Carlson's murders. He replied yes it is. Sheriff Burk was telling his deputy he was looking forward to spending time with Joshua in New York as to profile him. He continued to say he may be a good person for the crime, or maybe he is just a broken man whose wife left him! That is what I plan to find out by spending time with him in New York.

I expect you to keep up with the Carlson's case while I am gone and call me if anything changes. Deputy Carl assured Sheriff Burk he would make it his first priority. They paid for their coffee and corn muffins and walked over to say goodbye to Betsey and Joshua, who had been seated now, and said see you early tomorrow morning to them. Sheriff Thomas and Deputy Carl headed out to protect the town of Salem.

Betsey and Joshua finished their lunch as Nell came over to their table. Nell asked how the food had been. Great as usual, Betsey said. Nell asked about their trip to New York and felt slighted she had not been included! Betsey told her it happened so fast and was sorry she did not ask her to go as well. Nell accepted her apology and wished them a fun and safe trip. Betsey told Nell when she returned home she would fill her in on everything they did in the big city! Nell told Betsey that sounded great and went back into the kitchen to cook for her busy lunch crowd.

Meanwhile, Sahara was waiting for her lunch break to go clothes shopping as well. She had heard Betsey and Joshua were in town doing the same. Sheriff Burk, after leaving Nell's place, stopped and told her how he and Deputy Carl had ran into them in town. Sahara asked Thomas if he needed anything new to bring on their trip. Thomas told her he could and they arranged to meet after work to shop as well for their trip. Thomas said he really needed Sahara's help in the clothes department!

Sahara laughed as well as Deputy Carl did! Thomas said, "Hey,you guys do not have to be so cruel!"

Thomas agreed to meet her at the real-estate office at 5 0'clock sharp. Sahara would invite him back to the house for dinner, as she had planned Alexi's favorite dinner before leaving on her trip. She had Cornish hens marinating with white rice, walnuts, celery and cranberry stuffing for dinner. Sahara knew this would smooth over her news to her daughter about her leaving tomorrow and making her daughter stay at a friend's house for five days. Thomas told her he had already made reservations for dinner for the three of them in town. Thomas thought she would not want to cook with leaving in the morning. She was surprised and told him that would be great. She would send her dinner with Alexis to her friend's house for tomorrow's dinner there instead.

Alexis hated to be away from her mother for a long time after losing her dad. Sahara knew this but she needed to get away as she missed her husband very much so as well. Sahara was glad she finally could have feelings for another man, which made her love life again. In addition, she and Alexis would have a bright future. Sahara was grateful to Betsey for opening her eyes up to seeing how much fun she could have with Thomas. He was such a gentle man and shared the same interests as she did. Sahara was afraid of Alexis getting close with Thomas and then things not working out and breaking her daughter's heart. Sahara needed to push these thoughts out of her mind and work on this not happening. If things went, the way she wanted this would be a wonderful life for her and Alexis.

Sahara finished her last client of the day and waited

for Thomas to join her for their shopping date for new clothes for the trip. Thomas arrived five minutes early, excited about their trip. Meanwhile Betsey and Joshua had been showing Mr. Green what to do for the horses while they were away. Betsey then invited him to stay for dinner; he accepted so Betsey left him and Joshua in the barn and went up to the house to start dinner.

Betsey had marinated venison tenderloins this morning and needed to preheat the oven, and then sear the meat in a fry pan with olive oil, butter and sage. Then she would pour it in a casserole dish with potatoes, onions and carrots and bake for an hour. After finishing putting together her dinner she went to check messages on her phone. There were two messages, Bob the warden at James's prison and Attorney Thornton. Betsey was scared to call either one back; she could only think it was more bad news. Betsey decided to wait until she returned from her trip before calling them back. She had enough pain in her life these last few months to last her a lifetime!

Betsey needed time away before taking on more bad news. She cleared the messages on the phone and went back to preparing dinner. As Betsey lit the candles on the dining room table, she set the plates, napkins and silverware and went back into the kitchen to finish the meal. As Betsey went back into the kitchen, Joshua and Mr. Green were coming in the back door. She told them dinner would be another hour and for them to have a seat in the living room before dinner.

Joshua started a fire in the fireplace as Betsey opened a bottle of wine and brought two glasses for to them. Mr. Green loved the attention; he had been living alone now for two years. His wife passed away two years ago after

50 years of marriage. They had two children, which had moved away years ago after college. Mr. and Mrs. Green did not have much contact with their children even after their mothers passing.

Betsey knew this bothered Mr. Green. She had always tried to invite him for the holidays over the years due to his situation. He had always come for Thanksgiving and Christmas dinners and Betsey always was very happy he did. Mr. Green and his family went back to the 1920's in Salem. The farm Mr. Green lived on had been his great grandfathers before his father took over running it. Now three generations later he was still working the same farm. Mr. Green was a very private man but would be there for any member of Salem if they needed him.

They sat and enjoyed their dinner as did Mr. Green, as he did not have anyone cooking for him anymore. Betsey noticed he had cleaned his plate and had licked it clean as well. She asked Mr. Green if he could do her a favor beyond taking care of the horses. Betsey told him she had food that would go bad due to them leaving and could he please take it home to eat, so as it will not spoil. He said yes my dear I would be glad to help you with that! Betsey was glad he accepted and filled a bag with containers with already prepared foods. She also packed left over's from their dinner tonight.

As Betsy cleaned up after dinner, Joshua and Mr. Green went to sit in the living room with tea. Betsey finished cleaning up after dinner and joined them with coconut squares for dessert. They all sat and enjoyed the coconut squares and tea. Mr. Green was ready to leave when Betsey brought him the bag of food to take home. He was so grateful to Betsey for the food and told her not to worry about the horses; he would take good care of them as if they were his own. Betsey said she knew he would, that is why he was her first choice for the job! Mr. Green blushed as he kissed Betsey on the check and again thanked her for the food.

Betsey told him she would call him when they arrived home in five days. Mr. Green told Betsey not to worry, he knew what to do and everything would be fine and to enjoy their trip. "God knows girl you deserve it!" Mr. Green said. Betsey thanked him and said see you in five days. As Mr. Green drove from Mainstay Inn, he was glad for Betsey with having Joshua to take care of her and the farm. Betsey had always been sweet as a child and as an adult as well. After Mr. Green left, Betsey went upstairs to finish packing for their trip to New York City. Joshua was out in the barn checking on supplies that might be needed while they were gone.

Sheriff Burk and Sahara were all ready to leave tomorrow on their trip. As Betsey packed the phone rang so she ran downstairs to answer it. Sahara was on the other end asking Betsey if she and Joshua were all ready for the trip. Betsey told her just doing last minute packing. Sahara said how she and Thomas were ready yesterday!

CHAPTER 35

They agreed to meet at 5am at the farm and take one car to the airport. Jeff and Beth Martin were already in New York City; they had left last night for the big city. They were to meet up at the Hilton tomorrow at 2pm. When Sahara arrived home Alexis was packing to stay at her friend's house for the week. Sahara could tell her daughter was feeling a little disappointed on not going on the trip with her mother. Therefore, Sahara tried to talk to her daughter about her feelings on the issue. Alexis told her mother she was disappointed she was not going and would miss her mother very much! Sahara told Alexis she felt the same and would bring her something nice back from the city. Alexis hugged her mother and told her to have a goodtime and not to worry about her. Sahara promised to call Alexis two times a day, morning and before bed every night. Alexis hugged her mom again and told her she loved her and to have a good time again and be safe. Sahara told her daughter ditto to that.

Sahara told Alexis dinner would be at Indian West tonight. Thomas was taking them both out for supper. He would be arriving soon so she should go get dressed for dinner. Alexis was thrilled; she loved that restaurant. Sahara went into her bedroom to change for dinner as well.

Thomas arrived a few minutes early so he sat in the living room waiting as Sahara and Alexis were not ready yet. Sahara told him it takes girls a long time to get ready! Thomas told her she looked great already. Sahara blushed and thanked him but still had to put her makeup on and fix her hair. She brought Thomas a beer and said they would be right down. Thomas sat in the living room drinking his beer and was glad for him and Sahara meeting. She was a remarkable woman who had grace and style.

Back at Mainstay Inn Betsey and Joshua were both in the kitchen making plans together on things to do in NYC. They were roasting rabbit with saved pork gravy, onions, carrots, potatoes and herbs in the oven. It smelled wonderful and was about ready to take out of the oven. Betsey knew this would taste wonderful the night they returned home from NYC. They both sat down at the kitchen table and the phone rang. Betsey went to answer the phone as Joshua sat at the table wondering what else he would need to take care of to keep his Betsey. Joshua knew about her ties with friends and the town's people. This was a problem for him, as he wanted her all to himself.

It was Attorney Thornton. He was letting Betsey know a new trial would be set for the beginning of next month. Betsey was thrilled to know James would have a new trial. She told his Attorney she would be available for court in her husband's behalf. Attorney Thornton told Betsey he would put her on the witness list and tell James. Betsey thanked him and hung up feeling much better about things. Joshua saw the smile on her face and asked who had called? Betsey told him about her husband's new trial and that she would be called as a witness for his defense.

Betsey was hoping for the best. Joshua looked at

Betsey and said, "But he murdered two people Betsey!" She replied "in self-defense! James's new attorney thinks they have a good case. He thinks I will be a good witness for James due to knowing him as a child, and spending my life with him for many years now".

Joshua just turned his head away from Betsey and began to clear the table after preparing their home coming meal. Betsey stated she was not done with her dinner yet and continued to fill containers. She asked Joshua to sit and wait to clear the table. He poured himself another glass of wine and sat while Betsey finished. She asked him what was wrong.

Betsey could tell her phone call had changed his mood for the worse. As Betsey was finishing placing her food in containers for the freezer, she tried to have a conversation with Joshua with no positive response from him. He was very cold and despondent. Betsey asked him what was wrong again. Joshua said he was tired and they needed to be up early for their trip to New York.

Betsey helped him finish cleaning up the table and they both went to bed not talking soon after. Betsey knew something was very wrong, as Joshua did not kiss or touch her in bed. They both slept until the alarm went off in the morning.

Meanwhile, after coming back from town after dinner, Thomas and Sahara shared a romantic night in bed. They made love until the wee hours. When their alarm went off it was hard for them to get up.

Alexis had been up and showered and was ready for school and for staying at her friend's house. Thomas and Sahara took their showers together and headed downstairs for breakfast. At their surprise, Alexis had made scrambled eggs, bacon, and home fries and toast already. Sahara was surprised and thanked Alexis for doing this. Alexis just smiled and told them to sit down for breakfast as she served them. They sat and ate over conversation of how good Alexis could cook; she took after her aunt Betsey!

Back at the Mainstay Inn, Betsey and Joshua showered and brought their luggage downstairs for Joshua to put in the truck as they were driving to the airport. Betsey went into the kitchen and poured them coffee and made omelets with tomatoes, goat cheese and mushrooms before they left for the airport.

CHAPTER 36

Meanwhile Butch and Tom were landing at Logan Airport in Boston. They needed to talk to Joshua in person regarding him and Heidi breaking up. Betsey and Joshua finished breakfast almost in silence. As Betsey washed up the breakfast dishes, she asked Joshua what was bothering him again. He started in with how could you want to help James after how he has treated you! Betsey told him he still was her husband and she was sure he never would have committed these crimes if it had not been for self-defense! Joshua threw his hands up in the air and told her he gave up! With that said, Joshua went down to the ban to take care of the horses. Betsey slammed a cup of coffee on the table and sat down feeling terrible about how she has handled her life so far. After all, she was still married to James but sleeping with a man she has only know for months now. What was wrong with her? What could she be thinking!

As Betsey sat and pondered over her screwed up life the doorbell rang. Betsey answered the door; it was Sahara and Thomas ready for their trip to the big city. Betsey invited them in, and said Joshua was still down at the barn and they would be leaving soon. She asked them if they wanted a cup of coffee. They said that would be great, as they did not get much sleep last night. Betsey tried to break a smile as she handed them their coffee. She replied, glad someone had lost sleep! Sahara knew her friend well and knew something was wrong.

Sahara told Thomas to go check on Joshua, as she needed to talk with Betsey alone. Thomas grabbed his cup of coffee while Betsey handed him a cup for Joshua too. Thomas left for the barn with two cups of coffee. Thomas's gut feeling was showing itself again regarding something was not right with Joshua.

Butch and Tom were outside Logan Airport waiting for a taxi to bring them to the Sheriffs Dept in Salem. They needed to track down Joshua in person to get some answers. What they did not know is that the Joshua they were tracking was not the same Joshua Tripp!

Thomas had entered the barn to find Joshua throwing hay and talking to himself. All Thomas could make out was Joshua thought Betsey was crazy! Thomas startled Joshua as he yelled anyone here! Joshua stopped tossing hay and yelled who was there. Thomas came into his view holding two cups of coffee. Thomas said, he was told to go check on Joshua, as Sahara wanted to talk with Betsey alone.

Thomas asked Joshua if he wanted to talk about what was going on between him and Betsey. Joshua took a cup of coffee from Thomas and sat down on a bale of hay. He began by telling Thomas, I do not get her! Betsey's husband has killed two people within a few months and she thinks he is great. James has told her in no uncertain terms that he will not see her. I do not get it, what is she thinking! He is only going to hurt her again repeatedly!

Thomas asked Joshua what had happened to bring this situation on with him and Betsey. He said James's

Attorney called Betsey last night and asked her to be a creditable witness for James. Betsey said she would, as her and James grew up together. Joshua knew not to react too much about this to Thomas. He would be smart to keep his cool. As he knew, Thomas would judge him as a cop. After all, they had a murder case going on involving him and anyone close to Betsey might start looking at him. Thomas told him what Sahara had told him about Betsey and James. She had said she was glad Betsey had found you, Joshua. Joshua did not know how to reply to this. He finished feeding the horses and giving them water with Thomas's help.

They both headed for the house to leave for the airport. As Betsey, Joshua, Thomas, and Sahara drove to the airport, Tom and Butch were in a taxi heading for Salem. They reached the airport and checked in with an hour until takeoff for New York City. Meanwhile Butch and Tom arrived at Salem's Sheriffs Dept.

Thomas's cell phone rang as they were at their gate to board the plane for New York. It was Deputy Carl, calling to inform him there were two people at the station looking for Joshua. Thomas told Carl to question them about Joshua, and how they knew him. Also, do not inform them Joshua is on his way to New York City. Take them out to Joshua's house to make it look as if he is still in town. Sheriff Thomas asked Carl to get a search warrant for Joshua's house. Deputy Carl asked the reason. Sheriff Burk said the murder of the Carlson's. "No Way"! Carl replied.

He told him, just to do what he asked. I have to board the plane right now; we will talk later. All boarded the plane for New York City. Betsey and Joshua were getting along better now. As Betsey and Joshua took their seats, Joshua told Betsey he loved her and wanted to have a great trip. Betsey told him her as well! However, he needed to understand she still supported James no matter how he had disappointed her. Joshua's blood was boiling now! They took their seats on the plane and Joshua decided that in his best interest he needed to change his mood and try to relax and enjoy the trip. He could fix things later on their return to Salem.

Joshua all ready knew what he needed to do. To Save Betsey again by having James killed in prison. He had pulled it off with Attorney Carlson and could do it again. Betsey would be his forever as long as he was in control. Betsey looked over at Joshua on the plane and saw the smirk on his face, which scared her at times! Earlier today, he had been so withdrawn. So how could Joshua change his mood so quickly she wondered? As the plane was leaving the ground, Betsey grabbed Joshua's hand and held it tightly. Until the plane was up in flight and stable, Betsey held his hand, which Joshua enjoyed.

Meanwhile Tom and Butch were driving out to the house Joshua had rented in Salem. Butch and Tom never were told that Joshua had left for New York City with Betsey and friends. Deputy Carl pulled up in front of Joshua's cabin. Tom and Butch got out and could see Joshua renting this house. The view alone was amazing. It rather reminded them of home.

They went up to the front door and knocked on it. No one answered so they went around to the back deck and looked in the slider doors. It looked as no one was home so Tom and Butch headed back into town to find a place to stay. Deputy Carl dropped them off in town and instructed them on many places to stay pricewise. Tom and Butch were impressed with the town Joshua had picked to live in for now.

They were hungry and walked to Nell's place where they had heard was the best place for food. Tom and Butch made their way to Nell's. It was lunchtime so Tom and Butch had to wait for a table. As they waited, their attention was drawn to a conversation about Betsey and Joshua. Their ears were trained on the conversation. They began to try to get in on the conversation regarding their boss. Tom and Butch really needed to talk with Joshua Tripp. As they knew he and Heidi would never separate; they were sure of that if not anything else. They knew something was very wrong and needed to find Joshua.

CHAPTER 37

Joshua and Heidi had been meant for each other for life. They had worked for them for many years now and knew them well. They were finally seated, and ordered their lunch, as Nell came to their table to ask how they knew Joshua. News gets around Salem quickly about new comers in town. Tom and Butch told her the story of Joshua and Heidi Tripp. Moreover, how they knew something was very wrong, as Joshua would never leave Heidi, as well as she would never leave him.

This news was a total surprise to them that they had separated. Nell told them she did not know Joshua well, but knew he loved her best friend Betsey. It was apparent to her when they were together. Tom and Butch asked Nell were they could find Joshua. Nell told them he was away for a while and would be back in a week. Tom and Butch could not afford to stay a week and wait for his return. They ate their lunch, which was great, the waiter came to give them their bill and they asked to speak with Nell again. Nell came to their table and asked what else she could do to help them? Tom asked her if she might have a phone number for Joshua. Nell said she did and gave them Betsey's number. Butch and Tom paid for their lunch and headed for Salem's Inn to book a room for their two-day stay in Salem.

As they arrived at the Salem Inn, they were impressed with the hospitality in this town. They were outsiders but treated as family as soon as they hit the town. This could be why Joshua picked this town to stay for a while. It was like their hometown in Tennessee.

Betsey, Sahara, Joshua and Thomas arrived in New York City at 11o'clock am and got their luggage. They went outside to wait for their car. Jeff had arranged to pick them up and bring them to the hotel. As they arrived outside a man was holding a sign reading Mainstay guests. Thomas and Joshua went over to him and asked if he been sent by Jeff Martin? The driver said yes and his name was Carlos. Carlos told them to follow him as he grabbed their luggage and put it in the trunk of his limo. They all got in to the back seat and were on their way to the Hilton in style!

Meanwhile, Tom and Butch checked into Salem's Inn and were directed to their room. After settling in Butch and Tom went out to explore the town and find a place for dinner. As they walked the streets of Salem, everyone they met would say hi to them without even knowing them. Tom and Butch could understand why Joshua would want to stay awhile. This town was as if they were back in Tennessee. People were as friendly here as in their hometown.

As they walked towards downtown to the waterfront, they were amazed at the shops and cobblestone streets. Tom asked a passer-by if he knew of a good place to have dinner. He suggested to them the Victorian House on Waterfront Street. The prime rib was the best in town he said. Tom and Butch loved the sound of that and continued to waterfront Street to find the Victorian Restaurant.

Joshua had no idea of who was in Salem looking for him. They had just arrived at the Hilton. A staff member, who had great manners and humor, greeted them and escorted all of them to their rooms after they had checked in and he made them feel right at home. After they unpacked and dressed for dinner Joshua noticed there was a message on their room phone he went and played it. It was Jeff and Beth Martin welcoming them to their city. The Martins said they would meet them in the lobby bar at the Hilton at six o'clock. Sahara and Thomas received the same message as well.

Back in Salem Butch and Tom were enjoying a great dinner at the Victorian. Butch asked the waiter if he knew Joshua. Alex the waiter asked how Butch had known Joshua. Butch went on to tell him they knew each other for years back in Tennessee. Butch told Alex he was in town for business and thought he would hook up with Joshua while in town. Alex told him Joshua was just at the restaurant two days prior with friends; all were planning a trip to New York City. Butch remarked what luck, I am here and Joshua is in New York. Butch asked if Alex knew how long he would be gone. Alex told him he had no idea when Joshua would be back.

Butch and Tom ate their dinners and decided to walk around town after dinner. They thought maybe they could ask around town about Joshua and maybe find out where he was living for now, as he could not be staying out at the cabin. It had looked as no one was staying there right now. As Butch and Tom walked the waterfront looking for information on Joshua, Joshua was getting ready to explore the streets of New York City. Betsy was trying to find something to wear while talking on her phone to Sahara. She was checking with Sahara on what she was planning on wearing. Joshua was lying on the bed all dressed for the evening wondering what was taking Betsey so long! Joshua went to knock on the bathroom door as he overheard Betsey talking to Sahara on what to wear. "Women!" he said. He went and laid down on the bed to watch TV as he waited for Betsey. What he did not know was Butch and Tom were in Salem looking for their boss.

Betsey finally came out of the bathroom looking beautiful as always. Joshua was always surprised at how beautiful she was! Meanwhile, Thomas was waiting for Sahara as well. Sahara entered the bedroom and astounded Thomas! Sahara out did herself tonight. She could see in Thomas's eyes it had paid off. They all meet in the lounge downstairs.

Betsey and Sahara went on about how hot they looked, as Thomas and Joshua admired them. Betsey's cell phone rang; it was Nell. Betsey answered "hi Nell, what is wrong!" Nell told Betsy how two men from Tennessee were looking for Joshua. Betsey asked Joshua if he knew if anyone would be trying to find him. Joshua was stunned at first by the question! He asked Betsey whom she was talking with. Betsey told him Nell. She had two men asking about him. Joshua took the cell phone to talk with Nell. Nell told Joshua a Tom and Butch were in her restaurant asking about him. Joshua was alarmed by this news. What could he do to stop them; he was in New York City miles away from Salem.

Nell told Joshua they had said they would be in town

for two days. Joshua would not be back for five days, good! They would be back in Tennessee by then. As Joshua handed Betsey her phone back to speak with Nell the Martins arrived at the bar to meet them.

Jeff Martin could tell right off that Joshua was very uneasy about something. However, what was it! That was why he wanted this five day get away in his town to spend time with Joshua one on one, as to maybe break through Joshua's shield that he puts up.

Back in Tennessee, Sheriff Burk was back from his fishing trip and had seen paper work regarding questions Tom and Butch had about Joshua and Heidi. Sheriff Burk headed out to the Tripp Ranch to talk with them. As he arrived, he noticed the ranch was very quiet; no normal activity going on at the ranch. Sheriff Burk first stopped at the main house. There was no answer at the house; it was locked up tight. Apparently, Joshua or Heidi had not returned home yet, as the front door was always open when one of them was home. Sheriff Burk then drove down to the stables. The help hired by Tom and Burk to take care of the horses while they were gone greeted him. They told Sheriff Burk Butch and Tom were due back in two days from Salem. They had gone looking for Joshua.

Sheriff Burk headed back to the station to talk with his deputy Tom regarding what he had returned to from vacation. Deputy Tom informed him Butch and Tom was worried about the Tripps. He told them that Joshua was in Salem Mass. He also included how Heidi had left Joshua for another man. Sheriff Burk was surprised that Joshua or Heidi had not returned to the ranch as of yet. He was thinking something was not right as well. He could not believe the Tripp's could be apart this long. Sheriff Burk tried to call Butch on his cell phone. He only got his voicemail and left a message.

Meanwhile back in New York they were all walking down Time Square on the way to the restaurant for dinner. They needed to catch a taxi to the Tavern on the Green Restaurant for dinner. It was located in Central Park. As they made their way to Central Park, Joshua asked Betsey if she had heard anymore form Nell about the men looking for him. Betsey told him she had not, but why were men looking for him, it worried her. Joshua laughed it off and told her nothing to be concerned about I am sure just some old friends, that is all.

They dined at the famous Tavern on the Green Restaurant in New York's Central Park. The night was memorable for all! The food the best anyone had ever eaten. The dining room was unbelievable with vines and flowers covering the windows. It was a very romantic setting and all enjoyed.

As they sat and ate, Jeff asked Joshua why he had come to Salem to live. He told him he could have moved anywhere, but loved the quaintness' of the town of Salem and how friendly the town's people were to him on his first day in town. Jeff continued to ask Joshua about his life in Tennessee. Joshua told Jeff he did not want to talk about his life in Tennessee. Joshua told Jeff that life was over and that he had left behind many painful memories.

Jeff Martin knew he had a hard job ahead of him; Joshua was not being helpful so far. However, Jeff knew in his heart something was not right with Joshua whom he thought he knew. They finished dinner and took a walk through Central Park. All came upon a horse carriage and driver half way through the park; they all got in the carriage and took a horse ride thru the rest of Central Park.

CHAPTER 38

It was not like Joshua just to leave this way. Butch and Tom headed back into town to talk with the Sheriff. They both knew this could not be Joshua Tripp. Something was very wrong and Butch and Tom were going to find out what! Therefore, they drove to the Sheriff's office. As they arrived, they noticed two police officers from Texas entering the building. John Black was from Texas! What was going on here! Butch and Tom entered the building, and they were instructed to have a seat and wait for the commanding officer. Tom and Butch were wondering what had happened to John for a while now.

Commander David asked Tom and Butch to come with him. They were brought into the back of the station into a very small room and left there for hours. Both were getting frustrated and hungry. In addition, they would answer any questions the police had for them. They had never committed a crime in their life. They just wanted to find their boss and his wife Heidi. They finally got to tell the officers what had happened in Tennessee prior to their visit to Salem.

Officer Jake and Officer Olivia told them they would do everything they could to help them find Joshua Tripp. They informed Tom and Butch that he had committed no crime in their town. Tom and Butch needed some evidence for them to help locate Joshua at this point. Joshua had broken no rules as of yet in their town. From what they had heard, Joshua was a very rich man in town. Tom and Butch had to agree that was their boss Joshua Tripp as he was very rich. Butch and Tom were still not taking this lightly. They still could not accept Joshua and Heidi had split. Joshua and Heidi had been high school sweethearts from their first year of high school. They never would separate as far as everyone in their hometown knew.

Commander David told them sometimes friends and family are the last to know when couples are having problems. Butch spoke up and said not in Tennessee. Everyone knows everyone's business there sir. Tom and Butch thanked Commander David for his time and left to head back to Tennessee.

Meanwhile, back in New York City they all went back to the Martins flat for after dinner drinks in Manhattan. Jeff and Thomas again tried to ask Joshua about his life in Tennessee as the girls talked about Sahara's makeover tomorrow. Joshua told them his life was in Salem now and no need to talk about the past, his life was with Betsey now! Joshua excused himself and went into the bathroom to think about who could be looking for him in Salem. He had a good idea it was Butch and Tom.

Now Jeff and Tom are questioning him as well. As soon as they returned to Salem, he needed to make an excuse to go back to Tennessee. Joshua would have to get rid of Tom and Butch to finish all ties there. He would also have to find a man that looked like him and leave his body there as well so John Black would be dead as well.

This would close the case on Attorney Carlson and his

wife. The Martin boys had found the bag Joshua threw off the cliff and for sure it would lead back to John Black. Joshua reentered the living room to the girls chatter about Sahara's makeover. Beth was asking what Thomas wanted to change about Sahara? Thomas told her nothing, she was perfect the way she was! Jeff laughed and told him "nice move my man!" The girls all laughed. They finished their drinks and Joshua, Betsey, Sahara and Thomas headed back to the Hilton for the night. They decided to walk, as it was only six blocks.

They were amazed at all the people and traffic here. They enjoyed all the lights and TV screens in Times Square. Betsey and Sahara window-shopped as they passed the stores on the way. As they arrived at the Hilton, they entered the lounge for a nightcap before bed. Betsey and Sahara were meeting Beth at ten o'clock am for a day of spas, shopping, and Sahara's makeover. The men would be touring the business district with Jeff and then an Irish Pub for beers and burgers. Then they would all meet up at Rockefeller Center for dinner and more shopping.

Betsey and Joshua said good night to Sahara and Thomas as they all entered their rooms for the night. Betsey could tell Joshua was preoccupied by something and asked him what was wrong. He grabbed her, started to undress her saying nothing for her to worry about, and laid her on the bed. She laughed and said "have your way with me!" Joshua laughed as well and said "I will!" They made passionate love, it seemed for hours, before falling into a deep sleep. In the next room Sahara and Thomas were doing the same.

Morning came fast as the phone service made their wake up call at eight thirty am. Both couples took showers, dressed, and all met at the elevator to go down for breakfast together. They all were excited about their plans for today, except Joshua. He was not looking forward to spending the day with Thomas and Jeff. He really wanted to spend the day with Betsey. Joshua was afraid of more questions about his life.

Betsey and Sahara were still chatting as they entered the restaurant in the Hilton for breakfast. They were seated, poured fresh coffee, and given Danish before ordering their breakfast. Everyone ordered eggs Benedict. The Martins had said it was the best in New York. They drank their coffee and enjoyed the fresh Danish. Conversation was on what time they were meeting for dinner.

Thomas felt the same as Joshua; he wanted to spend the day with Sahara as well. The girls laughed and told them they loved to hear that but needed to get pretty for them. Joshua and Thomas said no need to; they were already beautiful! Betsey and Sahara both laughed and thanked them, but women like us will never be in New York again and Beth is pampering us! Really, how could we refuse! As that was said, their breakfast was served. All were amazed on how good it was. They all could not wait to see Rockefeller Center together.

Betsy, Sahara and Thomas could not believe Joshua had never visited New York City before. Joshua said he never had the need to come here. They finished their breakfast, paid the bill and started to walk to the Martin's flat. They arrived on time and Beth and Jeff were waiting for them. The girls went their way as the men headed for Wall Street. They were to meet up in Rockefeller Center at five o'clock pm. They were to meet at the Sea Quest Restaurant.

Back in Tennessee, Sheriff Burk was still trying to call Tom or Butch on their cell phones. Butch had forgotten to charge his phone and the battery was dead. Tom did not have his cell phone. Sheriff Burk was worried about the boys and decided to give Sheriff Thomas Burk a call in Salem to check up on them. Deputy Carl answered and informed him Thomas was on vacation, but Butch and Tom had been there and were on their way home. Sheriff Burk thanked Deputy Carl for his help and hung up. Sheriff Burk was more concerned now where Heidi Tripp could be. Things were not adding up. Heidi should have been home from the trip by now. Moreover, Joshua being in Salem Mass without Heidi didn't make sense to him. All he could do at this point was wait for Butch and Tom to return home and question them about what they had found out in Salem.

Jeff showed Thomas and Joshua Wall Street and was surprised Joshua had never been there, as how his family's holdings were worth millions. Joshua explained they were country folk and only did business in Texas. Jeff smiled and finally had a place to start checking him out besides Tennessee. They arrived at Muldoon's Irish Pub, sat at the bar, and ordered beers. After three rounds of beers, they ordered cheeseburgers' and fries.

The girls had just left the spa and were heading for the salon that Beth wanted to take Sahara to for her makeover. Beth and Betsey were getting a trim and makeup done, while Sahara was having a hair color change, perm, and her makeup done. From there they were going to Macys for new outfits for dinner.

The men finished at Muldoon's and were going to Jeff's men's club to play some pool while waiting for their ladies. Jeff also had to meet a client there to go over his pending court case. He figured Thomas and Joshua could play a game of pool as they waited for him to finish his business meeting. Joshua and Thomas were impressed at the fancy club.

Joshua and Thomas got a beer at the bar and went to play pool as Jeff had his meeting with his client. Meanwhile the girls were having so much fun at the salon. Beth and Betsey were done; just waiting for Sahara to be finished. She was just getting her hair blown dry. Her hair color was a vibrant blonde with red highlights. Sahara's perm was long curls like Betsey's hair. In addition, with her makeup she was gorgeous. Wait until Thomas sees her!

The three were now on their way to Macys for new outfits. Entering Macys, Betsey and Sahara were surprised by the size of the store and all the displays. Beth led them to the women's elite section. Betsey and Sahara had never seen so many clothes in one section of a store before. They would have a hard time choosing one outfit from here. Beth told them to browse while she went to get her designer to help them select the perfect outfits. Betsey and Sahara were impressed Beth had her own designer; that is why she always looks so great.

Beth returned with Kelly to help them with choosing the best dress to suit their personality and compliment their figures. They tried on many different dresses before finding the right one that totally complimented them. Next were shoes to match as well as a purse. After hours of trying on dresses, shoes, and purses they all looked good, enough to do a model shoot.

The guys were done at the men's club, and were going to Rockefeller Center to meet the girls for dinner. The girls were finished and stopped at the Hilton to drop off their old clothes at their suites before meeting the men at Rockefeller Center for dinner. Sahara was nervous, wondering if Thomas was going to be pleased with her new look. Beth and Betsey told her she looked sexy and Thomas will love you even more. Betsey could not wait for Joshua to see her new little black dress and ankle boots. She felt like a movie star all made-up with her designer black dress and boots!

Jeff, Thomas and Joshua arrived before the girls. Jeff went in to check on their reservation while Joshua and Thomas sat out front to wait for the girls. As they sat talking, they spotted three beautiful women walking their way. Joshua as well as Thomas could not believe their eyes. Their skin was radiant, hair glowing as their dresses hung on their bodies so sexy. They both stood up and approached the girls, excited to be with them. Thomas hugged and kissed Sahara as well as Joshua did Betsey. Jeff had walked outside the restaurant and embarrassed his wife as well, nice job babe he whispered in Beth's ear. She laughed and said thanks. They all went in and were brought to their table for dinner. They were seated below a huge fish tank, with sharks and stingrays and other colorful tropical fish as well. There also were mermaids swimming in the tank. On the menu, there was any kind of fish they could possible think of prepared by a famous chef. All ordered freshly prepared fish.

As they ate, the men remarked on how beautiful the girls all looked. All were very pleased with the meal and Jeff's choice on the restaurant. After dinner, they walked through the mall under Rockefeller Center going in and out of many stores with merchandise from around the world.

Then it was on to Times Square and to nightclubs for dancing. As they walked to Times Square Betsey started to feel very tired and nauseated. Joshua could tell by holding her hand something was wrong; her hand got sweaty and clammy. He asked her if she was ok. Betsey said she was starting to feel under the weather. Joshua saw a park across the street and made Betsey have a seat for a while. Sahara and Thomas were worried as Betsey's face was very pale and she was very shaky. Joshua rubbed her hands and asked her if he could get her anything. Betsey said some water would be good.

Joshua and Thomas looked down the street, spotted a food cart, and headed there to get her water. Sahara sat and held Betsey's hand while they went to get water for her. Sahara asked Betsey if she was all right. Betsey began to cry and told Sahara she was not sure. She was very late for her menstrual cycle, she cried out! Ok, Sahara said, we could handle this; we can handle anything together. Beth and Jeff Martin could not help to overhear Betsy's problem. They joined Sahara in comforting Betsey as well.

Joshua and Thomas returned with a bottle of water for Betsey. She drank the whole bottle in one gulp not stopping between sips. Joshua asked her what was wrong again. Betsey asked Joshua to sit down first before she told him the news that she might be pregnant. The others walked down the street to a shop to give Betsey and Joshua some privacy. Betsey looked into Joshua's eyes and blurted out that she may be pregnant! Joshua yelled at the top of his lungs "yes"! He hugged Betsey and could not let her go.

Joshua told her he was thrilled and would never leave her or their child. Joshua knew more now than ever he needed to take care of his past. His true identity, John Black. After all, now he was Joshua Tripp and was going to be a father. Joshua knew now he could not wait to return to Salem before leaving for Tennessee to follow through with his plan.

He continued to comfort Betsey before they continued to Times Square. After reaching Times Square Joshua and Betsey went back to their hotel, while the rest went on to the nightclubs for dancing. The talk was all about Betsey and her current situation. Sahara was thrilled for Betsey, as Betsey had always wanted children. The Martins and Thomas on the other hand were afraid for her. They did not trust Joshua if that was who he really was!

Betsey and Joshua arrived at their room and Joshua asked Betsey if she wanted anything from room service. She told him ginger ale and crackers would be great. Joshua laughed and said no better snack than that. "You got it sweetheart"! Joshua called room service, ordered her ginger ale and crackers, and laid down on the bed next to Betsey, the mother of his child.

Joshua was so overwhelmed with the news; he knew now what he needed to do! He would have to excuse himself and leave for Tennessee. Joshua needed to finish business there before he could go on with his new life with Betsey.

The first thing was to find a man that looked like him to take his place. He would leave his wallet and important papers on the body so that the body would be identified as John Black. He and Joshua had looked alike except for their eye color. He had been wearing contacts to make his eyes green like Joshua's had been. He had grown his hair out, as Joshua's hair had been long. Once he took care of Butch, Tom, and the stranger's body, he could live his new life as Joshua and be a father to his baby.

Joshua knew what he needed to do! He made sure Betsey was comfortable and told her business called him back to Tennessee. Joshua informed Betsey he needed to leave tonight and would meet her in Salem. Betsey, overwhelmed and maybe pregnant now, and Joshua leaving her in New York City, what was she to do!

Joshua called the airport for a flight out tonight as Betsey tried to reach Sahara to let her know Joshua had to leave. Joshua packed and was ready to leave for the airport, leaving Betsey crying and confused. He kissed her and her stomach. He told both of them he would see them in Salem. Joshua then told Betsey to have a good time in New York City, and he would be thinking of her and their baby.

CHAPTER 39

As he left the phone rang, it was Sahara. Betsey told her how Joshua had to return to Tennessee for business, which was urgent and could not wait for his return. Sahara told Betsey they would come back to the Hotel to stay with her. Betsey told her not to be concerned; Joshua had ordered room service for her and then she was going to get some sleep. Sahara understood. She told Betsey she would meet her at 9o'clock in the dining room for breakfast. Betsey agreed and told Sahara she would see her in the morning and also to have a great time out tonight dancing.

There was a knock at the door so Betsey went to answer it. It was room service with her ginger ale and crackers Joshua had ordered for her. Betsey ate and lay down to get some sleep. Betsey was so tired she fell asleep soon after her head hit the pillow. Meanwhile Sahara, Thomas and the Martins were at a hot spot nightclub in Manhattan. The music was different then Thomas and Sahara were use to. They seemed to enjoy the music so they danced many dances.

Sahara was worried about Betsey and let Thomas know what had expired between Betsey and Joshua this evening. Thomas told her if she needed to leave to be with Betsey he would understand and go with her. Sahara was thrilled to know he wanted to leave as well! She told Thomas that would be fine. They went to say goodbye to the Martins before leaving the club. Thomas knew Sahara was anxious to see Betsey after her news about Joshua. Thomas was ok with that as he was a family man at heart. Thomas knew this was going to be a hard time for Betsey, as for she was still married and carrying another man's baby!

They arrived at Betsey's room at 9:00 o'clock. They knocked and Betsey awoke and answered the door glad to see her friends. Betsey invited Sahara and Thomas in. Betsey went on to tell them how the pregnancy test had been positive and that Joshua had to leave to take care of business back in Tennessee. He would meet her in Salem next week.

She would need to tell James of her condition. This would be very hard for Betsey as her and James always dreamed of having children. Betsey was thrilled to know she was carrying a child. What she did not know was the child growing in her belly was that of a serial killer! Sahara and Thomas stayed for an hour with Betsey and then headed to their room for the night. They told Betsey they would see her at breakfast. The plan of the day for tomorrow was to go to the museums and have lunch at the Tavern on the Green in Central Park. They all enjoyed their dinner there and wanted to return before heading home.

Betsey was missing Joshua as they shopped and headed to Central Park to the Tavern on The Green for lunch. She wished he could be with her but knew he had business to take care of or he would be with her and their baby.

As they all ordered lunch, Jeff Martin asked Betsey were Joshua was. She told him he had business back in Tennessee that needed prompt attention so he had to leave last night to tend to it. Jeff asked Betsey how long he would be gone. She said one week. Joshua had said he would see her in Salem.

They all enjoyed their lunch; Betsey the most! She had ordered a club cheeseburger, fries, salad, fried Oysters and many different dipping sauces to go with all that. Everyone was laughing when Betsey placed her order.

Beth Martin had forgotten how much you loved food when you are pregnant. Jeff knew and the memories came back for him as how much food Beth had consumed when she had been pregnant. They all encouraged Betsy to eat as much as she wanted as you are eating for two now!

Meanwhile Joshua {John Black} was on his way to Tennessee to cover up his last murders and to finish off John Black forever. He had a great plan designing his own murder, as well as killing anyone else who got in his way.

CHAPTER 40

John Black's plane landed in Tennessee at 7:30 am in the morning. Joshua {John Black} headed for the ranch to see Butch and Tom, only though to kill them. First, he needed to search around town for a close duplicate of himself. When he had lived here and had come into town, he had noticed a man who looked just like him. He said to himself what a handsome man. Joshua {John Black} headed into town to search for this same man. He no sooner arrived into town and entered the main bar in town know as Break-Away-Point. As soon as he entered the bar, he noticed the man he was looking for playing pool. John approached him asking him to play a game of pool. This man asked who he thought he was interrupting his game like that! John told him he was just passing through town and said, "I was told to come here to see you for some action".

Then what is my name my friend? John stepped back from the man and said I am the asshole who is going to beat you in pool! Derek Jones stepped back and offered the table to John. He lucked out as another person in the bar called out to Derek. They wanted to know who was taking Derek's table. John asked if Derek had to ask permission to play pool with another man! Derek told John he would take him outside and show him he needed no one's permission for who he played pool with or anything else he did!

John had gotten the reaction he wanted from Derek but needed him to himself without all the on lookers from the bar. John leaned into Derek's ear and whispered "just you and me, man to man". Moreover, no interference from your heavy weights in the bar, agreed? Derek replied, "I will beat you in pool and beat your ass later!"

The game started with John winning.

Meanwhile back in New York City Betsey and the girls were shopping now for baby stuff. Betsey was feeling under the weather every hour now. They tried to shop around her morning sickness. Betsey was feeling very alone with Joshua gone and James in prison. They were all due to fly out of New York City at 5pm today. Betsey was wondering how Joshua was. As Betsey had not known that much about his past, all Betsey knew was she missed Joshua very much. She hoped he was ok as he was the father of her baby.

She and James had tried for years with no luck at conceiving. Betsey was not looking forward to giving the news to James regarding her pregnancy. James had made it clear he did not want to see or talk to her! Betsey was anxious to return to Salem to check on James' attorney. Betsey was looking forward to the new trial for James, as she never stopped believing in him or loving him.

Meanwhile Jeff Martin was checking in with the FBI office regarding updated information on the Carlson's case. To his surprise evidence lead to a man named John Black who had been released from prison one year ago for manslaughter among other charges. They had tried to get a profile and photo on him. To their surprise, there was none available. There had been a breach in the computer system and all information had been lost from 1983 to 1984 on several prisoners. Still, police now had a name to go with. Jeff left his office to meet up with Beth, Thomas, Sahara and Betsey for lunch. He could not wait to tell Thomas, if he already did not know! Jeff knew this would be good news for Betsey as well.

The Sheriffs Dept was that much closer to solving the case. When Jeff arrived at the Hilton Plaza, they were all waiting for him for lunch. Beth could tell her husband had good news just by looking at him. After ordering their lunch, Jeff told them the good news. Thomas took out his cell phone and called his office back in Salem.

Deputy Carl answered and told Thomas the new information regarding the Carlson case. Thomas tried to hold his anger as he informed Deputy Carl he had just heard about it in New York! "Sorry Boss, I was just going to call you regarding this. Hey, Boss how did you hear about it in New York", Carl asked. Thomas was very short with him and told him he would be home this evening and arrive at the office around seven pm. He ordered Carl to be there and have all the new evidence ready for him to review!

John had beat Derek in pool and now both were heading to the bar. Derek wanted to buy the asshole that beat him in pool a drink. John accepted, as this would work out better for his plan than going out to fight with him. Get the man drunk and make him your best friend in view of the other patrons as well. The bar was ready to close and John and Derek were still drinking, falling over each other as the bartender asked them to leave. John's plan was to follow Derek home and grab him there. As

John followed Derek home he had to laugh, Derek was all over the road with his pickup. Maybe he would get lucky and Derek would kill himself on his ride home and make it easier for him!

John had learned that Derek lived alone in a secluded area with no neighbors. This was in John's favor; easy in and out and no nosey neighbors to worry about. As far as anyone in the bar knew, John was heading up north to work on the oil pipelines. Derek parked his truck in front of his trailer and stumbled into the house not knowing he was followed home. John turned off his truck lights before driving up the driveway to Derek's trailer.

John sat and had a cigarette while waiting for Derek to fall asleep. Once he thought Derek was sleeping John got out of his truck and approached the trailer. He carefully opened the trailer door and went inside. He had known that Derek was very drunk and would not have locked his door. John could hear him snoring from a room in the back of the trailer. As he approached the back bedroom Derek stopped snoring. John stopped in his tracks, hoping Derek did not have a gun ready to shoot him. Then Derek started to snore again. John opened the door, jumped on top of Derek, and slit his throat. The snoring stopped and Derek was silent now.

John went into the bathroom to clean up, as his face was spattered with blood. He washed away all evidence of it and changed his shirt. He wrapped Derek's body and his bloody shirt in a shower curtain and dragged him to his truck. After loading him in the back of his truck, John took time to cook himself some breakfast in Derek's trailer before heading to the Tripp ranch.

It was now three am and another hour drive to the

ranch. John wanted to arrive at the Tripp's Ranch before Tom and Butch arrived for work. Surprise was the element he needed to pull this off! He finished his breakfast and locked up the trailer before leaving for the ranch. He knew he had to work fast as the rental truck was under his real name John Black. The the State Police would be notified soon as he would be wanted for murder and rape in Salem.

CHAPTER 41

John knew all the back roads to get him to the Tripp's Ranch and was making good time now as no one else was out on the roads yet. John arrived at four am at the ranch. There was no one around so he pulled his truck around back and parked it at the office door. John then waited for Tom and Butch to arrive. At five o'clock sharp, Tom and Butch drove up to the barn. They entered the barn and headed for the office to find John sitting at the desk. They both yelled hey John where have you been? We have been worried about you, as Joshua and Heidi are still gone as well. John smiled and said on a wonderful vacation that I do not intend to have end!

Tom and Butch just laughed and were glad he was back. They started to tell John they needed his help finding Joshua and Heidi. John had a smirk on his face and said, "sure, I will help you find them!"

He began to tell them he had noticed something was not right at the back door of the house when he had arrived. He told them the back door looked as if it had been jimmied open. They followed John up to the house saying they should call the Sheriff first. John told them to look for themselves first before calling the sheriff. They agreed and continued up to the house.

John had his gun stuck in the back of his pants as

to have it ready to shoot them both at the backdoor of the house. A robbery gone badly was the plan. As they approached the backdoor Tom and Butch took a close look at the door. Then John shot them both. They fell with a look of fear on their faces, which made John feel warm all over and it excited him. John then went into the Tripp's house and smashed things to make it look like a robbery.

John ran for his rented truck and poured gasoline over it, loaded Derek in the front seat, and lit it on fire. He dropped his wallet near the truck with all his identification as to identify the burnt body as John Black. It would be a closed case for his murders that he would soon be wanted for in Salem. John then took a horse from the ranch, as he knew the back roads that would get him close to the airport, as he needed to fly home to Betsey and his unborn baby in Salem.

What will the future hold for all! Their lives will take many twist and turns along the way in my next book After the Light.

With love to my husband and best friend.
I could not have done this without you!